RAIN IN THE SKY

M. A. COLE

RAIN IN THE SKY

Copyright © 2019 M.A. Cole

Dedication

In all three of my books in this series, I AM THE SKY, A SCAR IN THE SKY and now in RAIN IN THE SKY, there are definite truths throughout each. I did my best to wrap those truths around as much bologna as my imagination would let me. There is one thing, however, that's an absolute for me. I thank God so much for this experience. I'd also like to thank my family and friends, especially my daughter, Katelynn. My daughter has been the Mia of my life in many ways and so much more.

God Bless,

- MAC -

TABLE OF CONTENTS

Israel Rain

Not too very long ago
lived a man named Israel Rain,

He lived a life in many ways
full of struggle, strife, and pain;

Life made this man seek
a much needed enlightened path,

Ironically, it was his own little girl who rescued him
from a unforeseen deadly wrath;

Death itself couldn't stop his love
for the greatest treasure he ever knew,

Because God knew full well what each needed
*when **HIS** precious gift made her glorious debut.*

M. A. Cole

My Mia

I can't say that I've woken up from death or even that I know exactly where I am. I do know, however, that I have an almost overwhelming feeling of familiarity with everything around me. I feel like I've been here before even though I have absolutely no idea where "here" is. I was always told that after you die you should see some sort of magnificent bright light, and I do see a light, and it does seem to be amazing, but it's off in the distance and it appears to be quite far from where I am. I also hear, although faint, the most pleasant music.

That comforting hymn is so glorious that it's beyond anything that I could ever adequately describe with my own limited earthly comprehension. I think it's coming from the same direction as the light but I'm not really sure because it sounds like it's being delicately poured in from everywhere. If it wasn't for those two, what I can only define as heavenly signals, somehow engulfing me in assuredness, I would almost think that I somehow ended up in that other place—the one most commonly described as quite a bit hotter and possibly not so welcoming.

My instincts and that beautiful music are definitely telling me that I don't have anything to truly worry about, even though I'm trying to stir up my own emotions. I guess I'm doing this because, as I look back or somewhere else other than where I am, I can still remember with perfect clarity that I didn't have what most would consider an easy life. My middle brother, Sammy, who I was very close with died at a very young age. That was after he lived his own shortened life full of complications and not-so-ideal circumstances.

My other brother, the youngest one, Jacob, almost died during his youth as well. I also lost so many friends way before anyone would think their expected time should be. Many of those closest to me died in a terrible war. Some of them took their own lives and many others had their lives abruptly eliminated by whom we considered to be the enemy. Life just didn't seem to give me the cards that anyone could expect to win with. In response, I thought that death in the many ways that it presented itself was without question the unexpected and unwelcomed perennial theme of my earthly existence.

Admittedly, in many ways, my life resembled one of constant struggle, but in one very special way I will be the first to say that I was blessed beyond measure. I was truly just beginning to realize how much of a gift I was given, but for whatever reason I had to leave. I remember everything right now, right where I am, regardless of where that is, with perfect clarity. The prominent thought in my mind now is how my wife, Emily, became my ex-wife in a very short amount of time.

Before that happened, however, she gave me the most precious gift that anyone could ever receive. Whether I thought I was ready or not, she gave me my greatest teacher, my daughter, Mia. My own little girl regardless of her young age at my passing taught me some of my life's greatest and most profound lessons. Mia was such a great and unexpected gift to my life that I often questioned if I ever came close to deserving such a wonderful responsibility. Up until her birth I felt the only constant in my life was death, but not with her. She brought life, a real life, a life that finally made me feel blessed for having my own.

That little girl enlightened me about how great of a connection that kind love can bring. From day one, and in so many ways, she raised me every bit as much as I ever raised her. I don't think I ever fully realized the magnitude of this truth until right now. Right here in this place, I can still fully feel this eternal link to her. I realized I was gone in a sense, but I didn't feel gone from her. This is a connection that I pray is never taken away no matter where I am.

Not all fathers allow this acknowledgement but those of us who do fully understand that the bond between a father and a daughter begins at the first knowledge that such preciousness is in the womb. That blessed bond grows into a love that, for the sake of the child's safety, happiness, or even just for an innocent smile of contentment, will cause a father to do anything, to include lay down his own life, or, in my case, my afterlife, to protect my child or help her always be happy. As I stood there in a self-imposed trance pondering about what was and also thinking about what may be from this point on, my thoughts started moving towards three other very distinct realizations.

Tattoo Tribute

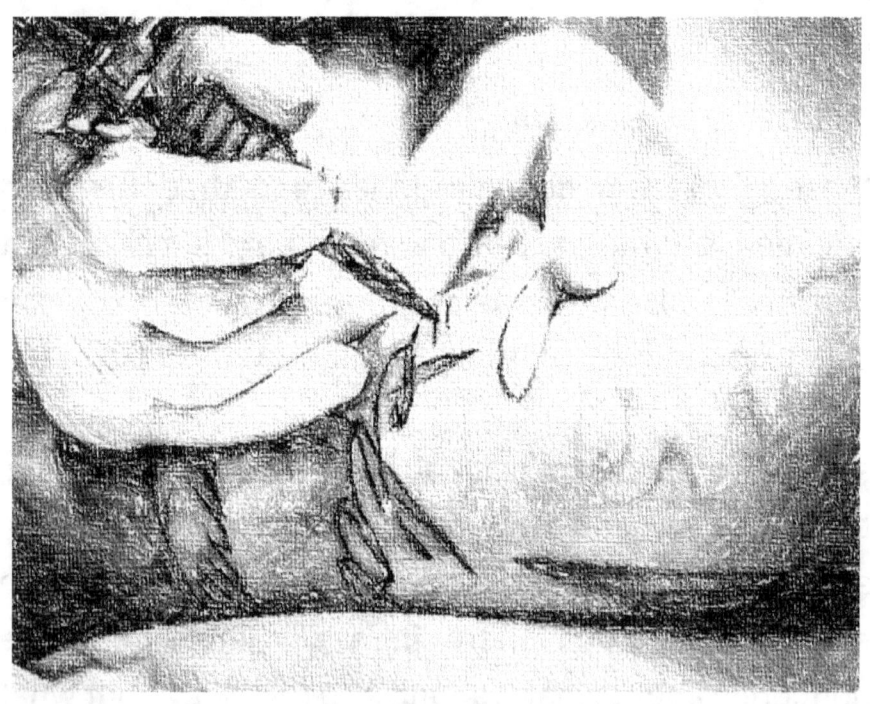

The first thing I noticed was there was some sort of path that was almost hidden and somewhat covered up underneath my flower garden-like surroundings. It nestled itself a very short distance from where I was standing, and it appeared to be leading towards where I thought that sweet music and the majestic bright light was originating from. The path itself didn't seem much different than any other that you'd see at a local park or in a well-groomed backyard, but it did seem to be strangely inviting me towards it for some reason.

It was like my body was being pulled towards it, but I stubbornly wouldn't let my feet or the rest of me move an inch in its direction. I felt as if I was in one of those dreams where you absolutely know with certainty that you're completely as awake as you've ever been, but you're not awake at all; you're just dreaming that you're awake. With those types of dreams, you can't move a muscle or snap yourself out of it either. I must admit, this self-imposed constriction gave me that unsettling feeling that I was only attempting to gain before.

What made those feelings worse was my second realization. This was something else that I was always told when I was alive but definitely wasn't experiencing in any shape or form for myself in this odd place. From an early age I was taught that, when you die, you are instantly reunited with your family and friends who passed on before you did. They are supposed to be the ones that you missed so much while you were left behind. What I definitely noticed now was I didn't see any of them. In fact, at this point, I didn't see anyone at all.

I was in some sort of motionless stupor in the middle of what looked like a gigantic flower garden all by myself. The more I looked around, the more it seemed like I was just standing in someone's backyard somewhere instead of anywhere I expected to arrive at in the great beyond. I still wanted to feel that there wasn't anything to be overly distressed about, but I still wouldn't allow myself to move at all for some strange reason. As my uneasy feelings continued escalating, my third and strangest awareness came to light. This realization was so odd but at least thinking about it took my attention away from the two prior, more serious realizations.

I got to the point where I felt so strongly that death was such a perennial theme of my life that, every time another person I loved died, in my youthful ignorance, I would get a tattoo of some sort on my right arm to serve as a permanent remembrance of them. I honestly felt that my heart was always in the right place in regard to my painfully inked arm memorial, but more so, I genuinely thought that I was giving those that I missed so much a lasting visual place in my life once again.

My justification for anything I ever did that was somewhat questionable always seemed to come to me from somewhere between a lie to myself and the actual truth. That self-prescribed rationale always gave me just enough courage and reasoning to help rationalize most of what my misdirected actions were, regardless of if I knew what the outcome would actually be. The problem with my well-intentioned memorials was and always will be that not one of those marks that I had chiseled on my body ever brought any of my loved ones back—not even once—in any way.

If anything, those tattoos often made things worse because every time I got a glance at my arm, whether on purpose or inadvertently, I'd often feel that pain all over again. The many tattoos I got over the years ended up representing my losses more so than anything else. Tattoos are complicated because they hurt, but at the same time, they are somewhat addictive. Every time I arrived at the tattoo parlor to get another to unfortunately add to my fleshy memorial, a big part of me wanted the physical pain. For me, it was almost a deserving punishment for my life continuing while the life of those I thought I was doing it for didn't.

Now, my third realization was, as unexplainable as it is, they're all gone now. As I looked down at my right arm, there was nothing there, nothing but unblemished skin. As a matter of fact, every scar or other imperfection that I may have visually had was gone too. My skin itself has changed to a more unified and humble shade of amber. It seems almost silky and much more regal. I really don't know how else to describe it because I've never seen that shade of purity before.

Now, for some reason, I don't have any tattoos, guilt or punishment marks. There was nothing but a naked arm, new skin and a lot of confusion about what's really going on with me in this place. I don't know why every time I think I know how something should be it never quite turns out that way. Life, and now death, have, once again, highlighted how little I actually know about anything. That's the way it was in my life and now, evidentially, it's going to be the same for me in death as well.

Miss Grace

Right before I worked myself up in a total tattooless frenzy, I started hearing something, or should I say, someone, whistling in the distance. At first, I couldn't see anything, but as the high-pitched tweeting became louder and more pronounced, I began to make out the silhouette of what appeared to be a little old lady. She was wearing a big floppy hat and dark over-sized sunglasses. Those glasses were so big that they hid half of her face. She slowly shuffled her way to me through what seemed like millions and millions of flowers.

As she came closer, all the flower petals that she was shuffling through made it look like there was a rainbow headed my way. They say this place has many mansions, and for a second, I thought maybe I was just dropped off on the wrong floor of one those places, because for the life, or death of me, I had no idea who this elderly woman was. When she finally made it all the way up to me, I greeted her with a cautious yet welcoming "hello." She didn't say anything back at first, she just slowly kept circling me as if she was looking for any unwanted scratches on a brand-new car.

That little old lady walked around me for what felt like a hundred times. I guess she felt that she had to thoroughly check me out before she'd offer up any sort of final approval. After at least five full minutes of this old lady invading way too much of my personal space, she warmly giggled and finally introduced herself as Miss Grace. She also said, "Hello, Grampy," and gave me a big hug. I may not have known her, but she sure acted as if she knew me, so I played along. I didn't have a clue why she was calling me Grampy, but out of respect for my much older inspector general, I kindly responded back again, and this time I told her my name, Israel Rain, and I said it loud too, to make sure she heard it.

I wasn't alone anymore, so being called by someone else's nickname didn't seem to bother me at the time but so much. This lady may have been old, but I have to say she had the warmest hazel eyes hidden underneath those extra-large sunglasses. Her glasses really were way too big for her face and crookedly pulled down on her nose too. It was almost as if she was trying to hide her eyes for some reason. It didn't matter though; I couldn't miss those pronounced golden rings around her delicately aged pupils.

She also had the most distinguished-looking white hair that was flawlessly tucked to perfection underneath that silly hat of hers. Her eyes, her rosy cheeks and her somewhat plump little body gave her what I felt was a genuinely trustworthy appearance. I guess my legs trusted her too because, before I realized it, we were both headed towards the path that I wouldn't let myself go to on my own earlier. I don't know if I expected guardian angels, St. Peter, or even seventy-two vestal virgins to meet me at the pearly gates when I made it here, but that's definitely not what I got.

Instead, I was tardily received by someone that looked more like one of the Golden Girls in a ridiculously floppy hat and over-sized sunglasses. I must admit, this situation was kind of funny because this little lady evidentially was really going to be my divine tour guide to God-only-knows-where. In this case, I felt those words couldn't be taken any other way but in the most literal way. After what seemed like just a very few steps on the path that Miss Grace led me to so easily, I suddenly saw this absolutely beautiful cast of light come over her.

Her skin was originally very similar to mine, but now, for her at least, there was an additional glimmer of light that softly spread to all of our surroundings. It wasn't a bright light, but it was just enough to let me know that there was something very special about this little old lady. The funny thing is that I actually thought I'd seen such a glow come over someone like that before. When I met my daughter's mother, Emily, I could have sworn that she had a very similar glow to her as well. It may not have been as pronounced or spread as far as Miss Grace's did, but I definitely believed it was a signal to me from above.

For my ex-wife, whether I was right or wrong, I thought that it was God's way of showing me who he wanted me to be with. In my opinion, this was probably because I was too slow to figure it out for myself. The hat that Miss Grace had on was still ridiculous and her glasses were still covering too much of her face, but her soft, beautiful, glowing appearance brought such a peace over me. It was a peace that permeated throughout my whole body and definitely reached every inch of my soul.

I guess I could only come to the conclusion that, this time, there was no denying that Miss Grace's glorious radiance was unquestionably real. Although I didn't know where we were going, we were definitely heading somewhere together, and she was most definitely leading our way in more ways than one.

The Tree of Remembrance

As we walked on the path for a while, she seemed to already know all of the stories that I was attempting to tell her. I thought to myself, *can this lady give me a break; I just croaked here for goodness sake*. She listened to me but was very selective with her responses. I still didn't know where everyone I was supposed to see was, and every time I'd try ask her about them, she'd quickly redirect our conversation towards more of whatever she wanted me to know about instead.

It was a little frustrating to be truthful, but I politely listened to her describing the many different flowers that surrounded us instead of what I really wanted to know about. She also kept calling me "Grampy" for some reason, especially when she wanted my attention directed back towards whatever flower or tree that she wanted to tell me about. Her voice was so nurturing that I couldn't be overly mad at her anyway. Besides, I wasn't even brave enough to get too snappy with a woman who had a definite glow about her and the only one who actually knew where it was, we were headed to.

Our walk seemed more like being on a treadmill than any other sort of path that I'd ever been on. With a regular path you at least feel like you're making some headway towards reaching your intended destination, but not with this one. This stroll felt more like it went on forever without us ever truly gaining any ground. I think Miss Grace sensed my frustration even though I did the best I could to hide it. Even though I still wanted to ask her a million questions, she told me that we had walked enough for the day. She then told me to go over in the field next to a specific tree and get some rest.

I immediately thought to myself *I wasn't tired, and I didn't want to rest either*, but again, I still wasn't brave enough to refuse the orders that were given by an old, glowing woman. I reluctantly, yet respectfully followed her directions and departed from the path to make my way towards the field that she pointed to and, particularly, to that tree that she spoke of. When I arrived at the tree, I noticed that she had definitely been there before I was and left a makeshift bed made out of flower petals for me.

I never thought anyone would have to take naps in a place like this or even that you'd ever get tired, but I was doing exactly both of those things. Lying under that tree made me think about my past life once again. When I was younger, my brothers and I would spend hour upon hour just lying on our backs pretending that the clouds were animals, cars, people, or even particular body parts of a woman. We made those puffy white canvases of our imagination into just about anything we wanted them to be.

As I laid there this time, I think I just wanted the clouds that I'd never expect to be looking at again to tell me something instead of me trying to direct what they could become with my imagination. The clouds never seemed to let me down, and as I drifted off to what I guess was the greatest sleep of all sleeps, those beautiful clouds didn't let me down this time either. At first, I dreamt that I was a young boy again. I didn't have a care in the world. I ran around playing with my brothers and our dog that Sammy named Puddles. In these visions, my parents and grandparents always seemed to be around too.

This was a lot different from reality, because in life, my parents worked almost all the time to provide for their three adventurous boys. We were nowhere near being close to angels back then either. I mostly had a wonderful childhood up until my grandparents and brother died. I was in college when my brother passed away and something inside of me just snapped. For some reason, from that point on, and for a long time afterwards, I just kept running away. I ran away to college. I ran away to a foreign country, and then, I even joined the military to solidify my attempts to run as far away as I could.

It took my youngest brother getting sick for me to stop running from what, in reality, were mostly the thoughts of losing my other brother. For me, those thoughts were more like hauntings. No matter how far away I ran, I just couldn't get away from them. None of that ended until I went back to where they all started— until I went back home. I eventually turned things around and became what I felt was somewhat stationary again, even though there would always be a certain very special part of me missing.

I managed handling those feelings by telling myself that Sammy was in a much greater place, doing much greater things. I honestly had to completely buy into that thought to get a handle on him being gone. I don't think taking a stroll with an old lady, glowing or not, down a flower-laden path was exactly what I expected for him, or for me either for that matter. As I sprawled out in the pile of flower petals that Miss Grace so kindly made for me, I mostly dreamt about all the wonderful things that occurred in my life, but I also clearly saw the not-so-wonderful things as well.

I vividly revisited the war that I was in for so long. I once again saw all my friends who didn't make it home. I saw some of the ones I absolutely loved take their own life, and I also saw many others die in so many other ways. One of my hardest visions from that night was that I could even see my own death, and later, my little girl's reaction at my funeral. My heart, asleep or not, was crushing as I saw her crying at my grave site. She was only seven when I left, and now her daddy is gone. This time, gone seems to mean gone forever.

It was happening again. I felt like I was awake and directly experiencing these visions in real time, but I wasn't awake at all. I don't know how long I slept under what I am going to call my own personal tree of remembrance, but when I woke up, the rest of me felt like my right arm now appears. I must admit, I feel refreshed and a little different too. I guess this is what being made anew means. Miss Grace was right, I did need to rest for a while, but that rest, I believe, was supposed to be more like a final goodbye to many of my earthly concerns.

I guess that nap had to happen so I could be cleansed for whatever journey may come. Possibly now I can truly realize that I may actually be in a much greater place, and, just maybe, I too am here to do much greater things. That nap was more like a release of all my leftover emotions from an existence that was no more. I didn't forget my life as it was, I just evidentially had baggage that Miss Grace knew I had to compartmentalize to continue on the path to wherever it was she was taking me.

An Unfinished Life

I don't know why I expected my death to be any less confusing than so much of my life was, but I did, and, once again, my expectations about how things were going to be were obviously very wrong too. The one thing that I was fairly sure about was that it seemed pretty apparent that, regardless of where I am or what I was ever doing, whenever God wanted me to learn a lesson he always provided some sort of teacher to lead the way. Similar to the first time we met, my current floppy hatted professor, Miss Grace, was approaching and, once again, her jovial and very much out of tune whistling gave her arrival away.

This time, as she did the last, she greeted me with a "Hello Grampy," and then let out a cute little mischievous giggle. *This lady is nuts*, I thought. I don't know who in the hell—or this odd version of heaven, or wherever I am—this Grampy is, but it was obviously someone that Miss Grace had a great adoration for, so I guess, for me, that would have to be enough for now. As we made our way back to the path to wherever, she asked if I felt like I had an unfinished life. Without hesitation I quickly snapped my response back by telling her that was absolutely the way I perceived my present situation.

Like with everyone else that I began to tell her about—my brother, my friends and family who died before me—I also felt the same way about their lives. The conversations of this day finally began to have some meat on its bones. I wasn't feeling sorry for myself. I wasn't mad either; I just didn't understand why any of those that I spoke about, to include myself, had to leave their lives and the ones they loved so dearly, and in some cases, in such a terrible manner.

Miss Grace seemed to listen to every single word that I was so trustingly confiding in her about. She appeared to be profoundly internalizing my words as if she was reliving it herself right there on that path with me. She didn't provide any overly insightful response to my remarks, but she was definitely showing signs of a true and deep remorse for my heartfelt confusion. Hearing my response, she became undeniably upset, so I decided to lighten up the conversation a bit. Glowing or not, I could see that what I was saying was reaching somewhere deep inside of her and it was hurting her more than I was willing to allow.

Her emotions were coming from an obvious and sincere caring for me and the ones I loved and lost. As we walked, we both just quietly looked around for a while. I had no idea what she was thinking about, but I knew that I didn't want to cause her heart any more anguish. I also didn't want to run off the only company that knew where we were going. It was never in my original nature to want to hurt anyone anyway. Even in the war I thought about the men on the other side and their families as much as I ever did about myself.

It's not that I have ever been an overly sympathetic person, but I did know that everyone that we came in contact with in such manner had a life story of their own. I knew that they had their own families, their own joys and their own sorrows, just like I did. I just didn't see how one side could be so different than the other, regardless of what classification world governments placed upon them. Make no mistake about it, I also saw evil, it just seemed to be mislabeled as many times as it wasn't from what I experienced. Back then, whether it was labeled right or wrong, I still did what I was ordered to do, and I lived with the constant guilt that always came afterwards.

I guess I'm seeing for myself that I left the world with the ability to feel a similar feeling. When Miss Grace and I started talking again, out of the blue she strangely said, "You know, I've always been with you, and I always will be too." I really didn't know how to respond to her because, like I said, I've never seen this lady before now. Even more peculiarly, I almost felt that she was saying those words for herself as much as she was for me. I think for some reason she was trying to ease her own guilt about something, even though I didn't know why or what it was.

I didn't think she was God, but because of her statement and the way she so strangely blurted it out, I had to ask to make sure. She let out another one of those cute little giggles and said, "Oh, heavens no, but I really have always been with you, and, like I said, I always will be too." I think this walk upset her so much because, even though I didn't know it at the time, she had a job to do and, very much like I did in the war, there wasn't the complete surety that she actually wanted to do it at all either.

My Sweet, Sweet Brothers

If nothing else, I surely felt that I'd be all rested up after Miss Grace once again told me it was time for another intermission of sorts. This second involuntary round of rest came with accommodations that were even more beautiful than the last. This time, instead of flower petals, there was a hammock that was tightly stretched out between two towering palm-type trees. Those trees stretched so high in the air I couldn't even come close to seeing their tops. They were so big it took the scales on their trunks to make them recognizable.

The hammock was made of these huge, fuzzy, auburn-colored leaves that warmly enveloped my body once I reluctantly decided to get inside. It was like an unfinished cocoon that purposefully left only a sliver of an opening for me to fit into. Its positioning seemed to be purposefully forcing me to direct all my attention to this beautiful waterfall a very short distance away. As I settled into the only place my swaddle would allow, I couldn't take my eyes off the glistening stream of water that was gently trickling into the pool of water at its base.

It was almost hypnotizing because, to me, it was another holy reference that I was still very much in need of. At a minimum, it was the next step in Miss Grace's planned cleansing and everything seemed to be exactly how she intended it to be. Once again, I don't know if I was awake or in some sort of Miss-Grace-induced dream state but, either way, as I laid there peeping through the small allowance in my hammock, I saw a stout young man dashing out through the back side of the waterfall. I can remember rubbing my eyes and pinching myself to see if I was dreaming or not.

By my own recognition of pain, I concluded that I was definitely still awake, or could at least feel the piercing pain from my pinch in my sleep. This young man was coming towards me and, unlike Miss Grace, he was getting to me in a hurry without a trail of rainbow flower petals. He appeared to be in his late teens at the most and he had flowing, dusty-brown hair like the actor in the Hercules movies. As he got closer, I became very frightened because of his eyes. That feeling that I once had of having nothing to fear instantly left me.

I believe I lived with the knowing that someday I'd have to pay the piper for some of the things I did in my life and this definitely seemed like it was going to be that time. His eyes looked like those straight from what you'd see in a horror movie, or where I didn't think I was—in hell. Actual fire was raging out of the sides of each of that devil man's eyes. The flames fluttered all around his face and very unlike Miss Grace's peculiar welcoming, this evil dude jumped at me as to solidify the danger that he was delivering.

I tried my best to fumble my way out of that cocoon thing that I was once so impressed with. I did finally fall out on the ground but that was only after it spun around a few times like what you'd see happen to the more ignorant characters on the Saturday morning cartoons. Once I got an ounce of my bearings back, for some reason, I started to tense up as if I was going to actually try and defend myself against this hell hound thing. Not very long after I began, my bluff was called. I didn't know exactly what I was thinking. I guess I thought I was going to die again.

This time, I thought fire eyes was evidently going to get me. As I began to think that maybe I wasn't where I originally thought I was, this inferno man started laughing, and the idiot said, "Naw, just kidding." I was all but trembling in fear, but his voice was one that was very familiar, like most things up to this point were to me. This voice, however, I hadn't heard in such a long time. Right in front of me, he changed his eyes. They were eyes that I have definitely seen before. Once my heart stopped jumping and started pumping somewhere around a normal pace again, I noticed by the way the man was moving his muscles all around that he wanted me to notice his chiseled physique.

Then, instead of calling me Grampy, as Miss Grace seemed to do all the time, he called me by my real name. "Israel! Israel Rain!" he yelled in such excitement. Then he gave me an ever-familiar greeting from the past as he said, "Good day, Israel." This young man seemed so happy to see me now that he put his flames out. He was definitely still laughing about how he literally just scared the hell out of me, but I was still as confused as I've been since I got to this odd place.

He grabbed me up like a sack of potatoes and gave me this huge bear hug. It was one that virtually took all the air out of my lungs in a hurry. I just saw this guy's eyes on fire, so I was extremely uncomfortable to say the least. I didn't care if he was just kidding or not; I've never seen any crap like that before. He held me so hard that my feet actually came off of the ground and I honestly felt like my face was turning blue from a lack of oxygen. As I separated from his massive grip as politely as I could, I moved my head back away from his and looked directly into his eyes. First, I was just making sure he wasn't going to blow my face up with those fiery devil eyes, but, secondly, because I had to signal to him, that was enough hugging, man.

It was then that I knew who he was without a shadow of a doubt. I didn't know how it was him and I didn't know how he made his eyes do that crazy fire thing. I also didn't know how he looked the way he did now, but I knew it was him. I may not have recognized all the changes that he evidentially collected somewhere behind that waterfall, but I'd never forget the beautiful, loving eyes of my middle brother, Sammy.

I've missed those eyes and the rest of that boy so much. It was my sweet, sweet brother, Sammy. Once he knew that I knew it was him, I don't think either one of us wanted the next hug to end. After the hug and our own joyous waterfalls of joy finally stopped, Sammy held his arms up in the air and flexed his muscles up and down, and proudly said, "Look! Look, Israel! Look at me now!" You see, in life, my brother was the most precious person I've ever known. He loved everyone and everyone loved him too. Just by being himself, he'd light up any room he ever entered. I truly think the room itself would miss him after he left.

He also always had this strange greeting and farewell for some reason. He'd say, "Good day" to every single person he ever met. I think he saw it in some movie, and once he did, he never stopped paying it forward. The funny thing is our whole town adapted his unique salutation. They did it when he was alive, and it definitely grew even further throughout our town after he died. I guess it was out of respect and admiration for such a wonderful young man who also left life in what we all thought was a time way too soon.

Even though I'd never seen Sammy act any other way than happy throughout his entire life, now his contentment and joy was at a level that was indescribable. It was one that I felt was most deserving. You see, when Sammy was alive, he lived with Down Syndrome, but not now. Now, Sammy's body resembled someone more like a reincarnated, slimmer version of the real Hercules. It was also a body that he was definitely proud of and one that he kept showing off by flexing up and down at me. It was like we were never separated once the original shock of his new appearance wore off—that, and when he extinguished those stupid, scary eyes.

Sammy and I were always close and shared many of the same hobbies in life. We both loved fishing and art projects of any kind, especially painting. I enjoyed painting so much that I eventually went to college to pursue an art degree. Sammy died while I was there, and my life spiraled out of control afterwards. I could barely handle him being gone, but he's not gone anymore, not from me anyway. I thought to myself, *finally, I may really be in the right place after all, even though Sammy and his eyeballs jokingly tried to make me feel otherwise.*

Sammy and I never had any problems with communicating with each other and we didn't on this occasion either. I knew that I could ask him anything. I also knew he would always tell me exactly how he thought it was with that same innocence as he always did. This was what I needed, and much more along the lines of what I expected in a place like this, but so much better. Even though many don't realize it, there's an absolute beauty to Down Syndrome. Most people don't get the privilege to see or experience this blessing but there's such a purity and wholesomeness that it surprisingly brings. Sammy still has that and so much more now.

A Higher Frequency

We sat on the rocks near the waterfall talking about our parents and grandparents and how wonderful of an upbringing we felt we had for quite a while. We talked about our other brother, Jacob, and all the trouble we used to get into as children as well. We also talked about my greatest blessing, Mia. I asked him about where we were and what was going to happen next. He let me know that where I was, was more like a life in between lives—in his words, I was in the middle, so I just needed to deal with it. He told me that this place was most likely temporary if I chose for it to be, but very real, nonetheless.

He then sarcastically told me he lived at the destination and assured me that, with time and patience, we'd most likely be roommates once again. I didn't know if that part of the story was good or bad, but either way, he disclosed that I'd only be given a little at a time, and this life in between lives is like the last life in many ways. There may be times that aren't always easy, but it would most definitely be worth it at the end of the journey. He then, as he had been ever since we reunited, flexed his muscles up and down and all around once again.

He wanted to make sure that I saw him doing it each time too. Once he finally stopped playing around with his new body, he pointed to the pool of water at the base of the waterfall as to signal for me to look down. He told me it was just like tuning the rabbit ears of an old television set. We had to find the higher frequency, as he called it, to get the picture. According to Sammy, this higher frequency gave us the ability to see all the people we knew and loved, no matter where we were. He told me that, with the right frequency, we could see, hear, and in some cases, even interact with those who were still alive.

Sammy's directions worked too. I couldn't do it myself yet, but he could, and he showed off at that too. It was as if we were watching a movie screen draped across the pool of water at the base of the waterfall. He tuned into our parents and later he tuned into our other brother, Jacob, and his family. We also saw our friends and those who were such a big part of our lives from our past. Who I wanted to see the most, Mia, was nowhere to be tuned into though. I asked Sammy about her and he assured me that she was fine, but it wasn't time yet— I wasn't ready for that, in his words.

Time is a funny thing in this place; it's like it's barely moving here but jumping around for those still there. Also, the events that are happening in their actual time are much clearer for us to see than their past or future is. We can still sometimes see their past and future but it's quite fuzzy compared to their current time. I was happy to see everyone, I really was, and everyone looked like they were getting along as great as they could, but who I really wanted to see the most was Mia. Sammy, in his efforts at getting my mind off not being able to see her, asked me if I wanted to mess with Jacob.

This really was like old times where Sammy and I would team up in hopes that we would come up with something at Jacob's expense. In truth, Sammy always played the middle and sided with both of us. By doing so, he was the only one who actually ever won. When we were younger, Jacob and I fought a lot. He'd hit himself and then hide in the closet. He'd do that right before my mother came in the front door so that when she entered the house, he'd jump out and blame me. I'd get my butt beat, every single time he did that, so messing with him now sounded very appealing.

Doing things like jumping out of the hall closet, pretending that I hit him along with a hundred other similar instigations made me retaliate in some pretty creative ways. I shot him in the butt with a bb gun. I threw an oar over the house that knocked him completely out. Those kinds of reactions, along with so many other acts of retaliation, made for an extremely colorful childhood for all of us, even if the colors were often black and blue. Every time Jacob did something, I'd try to return the favor tenfold. This unruly behavior went on basically until I left for college.

I always loved both of my brothers, but my relationship with my youngest brother was nothing like what Sammy and I shared. Jacob and I tolerated each other at best until he got sick himself. He's okay now and, with time, we actually became as close as any hardheaded set of brothers could, but, once again, God only knows what Sammy was playfully stirring up to do to Jacob now. When Sammy "tuned into" Jacob in efforts to enforce some not-so-divine intervention.

We happened to catch Jacob the clearest as he was reading a bedtime story to his children. We listened carefully to see if what he was saying would give us any ideas about our next move. We were just like our old, immature selves as we were as kids but, this time, I didn't think we had any chance of our mother catching us. We even became a bit giddy thinking about the extreme upper hand that we had on Jacob this time. We were honestly getting excited about doing something that we knew we shouldn't but definitely were going to do anyway. Just like with the tattoos of my past, my justification, even here, was still somewhere between the truth and a lie to myself.

Just like times of old, I had Sammy, the other little trickster, to help influence my agreement with the plan. As Sammy and I mischievously listened in, we heard Jacob slightly adjust the words to a book he was pretending to read to his children. He replaced what was actually written with some of the true stories about him and his eavesdropping brothers. He used different names, but Sammy and I knew who he was so lovingly telling his children about.

Jacob, in his own way, was telling the actual stories from he and his brothers' shared pasts. Jacob started out by speaking about three fisherman who were attacked by a fierce pirate ship named the Armageddon. Immediately, Sammy and I started laughing because there was more truth to Jacob's story than his kids would probably ever know. In fact, when we were younger, we did have a small boat that was completely ran over by a much larger boat named the Armageddon one day while we were fishing. It ran over our little boat and all of us inside of it too.

The more Jacob spoke to his children, the more the sometimes-unbelievable true tales of our childhood came out. After a while, we could tell that Jacob was simply telling stories about us to his kids because he was obviously still missing his two older brothers pretty badly. Jacob was always more like our father than we were. He was a little more serious and usually a lot more responsible than we were too. He was definitely much more selfless than at least I ever seemed to be. Now he has a family of his own and he's still the same with them too, if not more so.

In his stories, he was simply giving one of the kindest, most loving secret eulogies to two more of his own loved ones who seemed to leave his life way too early. After seeing Jacob barely be able to make it through his own stories and hearing his loving words, I guess Sammy and I thought he deserved a little reprieve from whatever we may have thought we were going to do to him. That glimpse of Jacob's life made our hearts feel somewhat weighted because we could tell how much Jacob loved and appreciated his children, just like our parents did us, but also how much Sammy and I meant to him.

In a way, it felt like a million years ago, but in another, more special way, hearing those stories the way Jacob told them made it feel like they happened just yesterday. After we "untuned" to Jacob, Sammy hugged me way too tight again. He assured me that we'd see each other very soon, and, once again, said "Good day." As quickly as he appeared, he gave me one more ridiculous flex for the road and a big smile, and was gone again. My very, very special brother went back through that heavenly waterfall as quick as he came.

It made perfect sense to me that Sammy would have something to do with water in a place like this. I knew it was holy, but now it's more holy to me than I ever had the ability to know about before now. My heart was full, really full, and for the first time since I got to this place—and probably as I should have done from the beginning—I thanked God. I thanked God so much for both of my brothers and for the blessings from this wonderful day.

Tattered Wings

After Sammy disappeared behind that waterfall, a great feeling of appreciation consumed me. I must admit, I couldn't always manage those types of feelings well before, with one very cute exception. Mia changed that part of me. She gave me the ability to feel happiness and contentment again. This feeling, similar to what she revived in me, was a feeling of extraordinary appreciation. Sammy looked so happy and he was healthy too. I don't think he ever missed out on anything from having Down Syndrome other than living a longer earthly life. In fact, I honestly believe in many ways his life was more like life was intended to be—happy—really, really happy.

Now for him it's even better than either one of us ever expected it would be. Sammy looked great, but he also taught me a very important lesson during his visit— one I hoped to learn for myself in a very short time. I don't know whether it was on purpose or not. It may have been his way of looking out for his big brother once again, but he did teach me that everyone seems to have a frequency, and, evidentially, it was an energy that I had to learn to tune into. It was the way that I, in some way, could see and hear my Mia again.

Before I got too wrapped up in Sammy's tutorial, incidental or not, I began to hear a terrible fluttering noise coming down from the sky. It sounded like it was coming from somewhere near where I would think the tops of those huge trees would be. As I looked up this time, I didn't see fiery eyes, thank goodness. I wasn't scared for my life either because this time it was an angel, an actual angel like so many people have on the top of their Christmas trees. It was coming in with its wings plumbed out just like the tattoo I got on my arm after my old boss died in the war, but these feathers were real.

This angel, however unlike any I have ever seen inked on myself or in the movies, appeared to be beaten up and tattered, as if he himself just returned from a war. He wasn't scary-looking though, he looked honorable and proud. When he landed, I stood at attention as if I was back in the military for some reason. I don't think I knew what else to do and that kind of came naturally. As I was standing there with my arms and legs locked in place, several other angels came down behind the first one. Unlike the larger original one, the followers were completely clean and glistened from the light in the distance.

It looked like they had the same kind of new skin that I did. They looked more like what I thought an actual angel would look like. This time, however, regardless of any wings or ruffled appearance, I fully realized who he and the others were almost immediately after everyone settled in. Unlike Miss Grace, or when I didn't originally recognize my smart aleck brother with those stupid fiery eyes, I knew who these very welcomed visitors were. It was Sarge, and behind him, my other buddies who died in the war.

At first, I was somewhat apprehensive at the feathers and their general appearance, especially Sarge's, but I couldn't help myself. I broke rank and ran over to each one of them as if I were a lost child who had just found his family again. I hugged each one as hard as I could and almost as hard as Sammy hugged me. He had more of those new muscles than I did, so that comparison was a bit unfair, but I think this time Sarge and the other guys were probably thinking, *okay, that's enough, man*, but I couldn't help myself. All these men looked the exact same as I remembered, with some very definite exceptions.

In life, Sarge, who I strongly considered my second father, was a black man and, of course, he didn't have tattered wings or the ability to fly to my knowledge either. I never really thought about it before, and the only reason I did now was, well...he wasn't black anymore and neither were a few of my other friends who used to be. Just like the tattoos that riddled my right arm before my arrival, my color, my shade and my pigment were all gone, and so were theirs. It was all anew for all of us.

I have as much respect and admiration for Sarge as I've ever had for anyone. He was a good man that definitely had some terrible things happen to him, and in response, he did a pretty terrible thing to himself as well. Sarge was not only our father away from home, he was also the actual father of five boys of his own back home. We always thought he had a wonderful marriage, but while we were deployed, evidentially, his wife didn't feel the same way. The military did to his marriage what it often does, and once he found out that she didn't want to be married to a military man anymore, he killed himself on Christmas day. He did it with an M16 that we ironically decorated as a makeshift Christmas tree in the tent we all lived in earlier that day.

Along with my grandparents and brother, his death was one of the hardest losses of my life. I love that man and, even after his death, he somehow kept saving my life over and over again. As strange as it sounds, during my most trying times he was always there. After I personally saw his own life end, he spoke to me in the wind, he visited me in my dreams and he persistently sent me small but very effective reminders that I originally thought were just coincidences to let me know he'd always be there for me. This wonderful man saved my life over and over again, even if he or anyone else could save his.

There is a common belief about what happens to someone if they take their own life, and after seeing him, I now realize that love put him in that position, and I guess love must have also gotten him out too. He then held me by my shoulders and looked me directly in the eyes as a father would do. He then said, "Look what we have here, Rain in the sky." Sarge then let out that same old barrel laugh that we used to hear so often from him. He knew that I knew what he was talking about. He was talking about how, on one fateful day in one of first years in the military career, my dumb self fell off of a building.

While I was falling in my drunken adolescent stupor, I yelled out, *"I AM THE SKY!"* This intoxicated ignorance was something that he never let me live down, not even in this place, evidently. As he was trying to stop laughing and regain his composure, I made my way around to my other friends who just wanted to come out to see me before going back to wherever it was in the sky they came from. That left just us, a father and his son, alone to talk. Sarge smiled as he let me know that he noticed there were no tattoos or blemishes on my body. He then moved his own arms around and said, "See, I already knew we were all alike anyway."

Make no mistake about it, Sarge was rightfully proud of his heritage, but even more so about the confirmation of what he always knew and often taught us. Our outer appearance was now unmistakably seen as a true and holy commonality all the way around. It was just like our insides always have been, whether some would ever admit it or not. The real beauty of our new attire was how strongly it signaled the "oneness" with something that is so much greater than any of us could be on our own as individuals.

Sarge stayed for a while longer. We laughed and we cried together, and as Sammy did, he assured me that we'd see each other again and began to leave. I was so grateful that his blessed visit reminded me about just how much that man helped me after his own death. He spoke to me in the wind, he visited my dreams, and he persistently sent me small yet very effective reminders that I originally thought were just coincidences. If he could do that for me, there had to be a way for me to learn how to do the same for Mia. Before he left, I had to know why he looked the way he did. I respectfully asked Sarge why he looked so beaten up compared to the others.

I already had an idea of what could possibly be the reason, so I was somewhat scared that he was going to say it was from some sort of punishment or something like that, but he didn't. He just proudly winked at me and said, "Saving souls like yours, 'Rain in the sky,' is hard work, and I guess I wear my work on my new sleeves." He then, as strange as it is to say, flew off. What a beautiful man, and what a great gift to be allowed to see my friends and my second father once again. I then did the only thing that I knew to do, and I thanked God so much once again.

My Nanny and Papa

I definitely didn't want to rest or go to sleep at this point. I couldn't stop smiling about how Sammy's silly self tried to scare the hell out me as he and Jacob did so many times when we were younger but even better with those eyes. I have to admit that fire thing worked too because I was definitely scared, and he knew it. I was also thinking about my visit with Sarge and the guys flying around in the air with their new wings just a flappin', and, of course, I thought about Sarge's subtle wink as to tell me "Rain in the sky, I still got you."

I was so grateful but there were still other people that I wanted to see, especially my grandparents who I felt had to be in this place somewhere too. I was the oldest grandchild and I had a very special relationship with them. As far as people go, my grandmother and grandfather couldn't have been any different from one another. My Nanny, as me and my brothers called her, could chew us out for something I'm sure we did, but for some strange reason, we'd feel better afterwards. She must have had that loving correctional gene that none of the rest of my family seemed to inherit.

She had the darkest hair all the way up into her later years and she had eyes that were every bit as beautiful and nurturing as Miss Grace's were. She was a rather small woman herself in contrast to our grandfather. Papa, as we called him, was a huge man. He was more like a gentle giant in many ways, but he was also quite a bit of a task master as well. He liked things his way and that was it. It's not that he couldn't bend at times, it's just that he rarely did. The thing that both of my grandparents had very much in common was the love they had and showed for their entire family.

When I was younger their house was my favorite place to go—over the beach or the mountains or anywhere—I just wanted to go to Nanny and Papa's house. As I became a teenager and started doing my own thing, as teenagers do, I for some regrettable reason forgot how much I loved being around them and I didn't see them as much. It wasn't too long into my teen years that I heartbreakingly realized that I wouldn't get a chance to anymore either.

My Nanny died first and then my Papa. That big, old, tough man didn't live much more than a month after she passed away. He let us all know that he didn't want to live without her either. With all the death that surrounded me in my life, they were the first two and some of the most painful to experience. As a teenager I was definitely one of those kids who believed my grandparents would live forever, but as I'd learn so many times afterwards, life and death both usually have their own plans and there is very little anyone can really do about it.

When I went to both respective funerals, I made sure that I held each by the hand as a final goodbye. It was my way before tattoos to try to remember something that I felt I could keep with me forever. I didn't ever want to forget the hands that provided so much love to me and my family throughout our lives. My Nanny's hands were small and soft. When I held hers in mine they still seemed to be as warm as they ever were. Not even death could diminish the warmth that her heart so lovingly and consistently produced and gave to her family so graciously.

When I held my Papa's hand, mine in comparison to his was still as small as it ever was when I was a little boy. His hands were not only powerful but also chaliced with several mangled fingernails that were a clear-cut reminder to all of us of how hard that man worked throughout his life to provide for his family in his own way. I knew I would always need that gutsiness that his hands helped create. No matter wherever I was, whether in college, the military, at another funeral, anytime I needed my grandparents I could close my eyes and feel the love that my grandparents and their hands provided.

I can still do it now. I don't know why I chose their left hands to hold. It may have just been the closest to me at the time, but just maybe it may have been the one that I thought was the most direct path from their hearts to mine. Either way, with my eyes closed tight I felt them with me once again. I think maybe this is as close to that tuning in that Jacob was talking about because now, not only can I feel their hands, I can also see both of them right in front of me.

Much different from the last very-appreciated visitors from my past, my Nanny and Papa were almost translucent. Not ghostlike or scary but more comparable to a loving spirit. My Papa's body may have been semitransparent, but his hand surely wasn't as he used one of his massive paws to bop me on the back of the head. He then laughed and said, "Boy, what are you doing?" as if I just woke him up from a nap or interrupted his dinner. Just like when they were alive, my Nanny started fussing at him and said, "Don't hit that boy in the head" as if it could still hurt me now.

It wasn't ever an aggressive slap; it was just a little grandfatherly welcoming that he loved to give and that my Nanny absolutely hated seeing. I think he did it to mess with her as much as he did to toughen me up. They too had changed in one way but not in another. They were very recognizable but in a younger, smoother, non-descript skin sort of way. Their faces that once carried lines and wrinkles of aging were now smooth and clear. My grandfather jokingly rubbed his face and sarcastically asked me how I liked his new digs.

The funny thing about all of the visits was—maybe with the exception of the fiery eyes—everyone's skin, the wings of my friends, and now my grandparents see-throughness. All the interactions like the path that Miss Grace was leading me on were very much like what we would have had back at home. It was kind of a blessing because, although strange at times, nothing ever really felt overwhelming. It was as if my experience was preplanned in regard to what I could actually handle and when I could handle it.

During my grandparents' visit, I could almost swear that she wanted to talk about whether or not she wanted to bake a pie. If she actually did, she held off because they mostly talked about how proud they were of me and my brothers. I didn't think my heart could become any more full, but if anyone could have maxed it out, it would definitely been my grandparents. They also let me know that, before long, I'd have some pretty big realizations to deal with, and in their seasoned wisdom they reminded me that free will was invented in this place, so I had better use it wisely.

Just like all the others, they began to leave to wherever it was that everyone goes. Before they totally disappeared, my Papa called me over as if he wanted to give me one last hug. As I ran over to him as I would have when I was a child, I should have known better. Even in this place that wasn't the case and another bop on the back of the head and chuckle is what I got. He deservingly got fussed at again by my Nanny though, so it wasn't too bad. With them, they'd never say a regular goodbye either. They had a unique farewell of their own. They'd always say, "See ya later," and this time they kept their promise from the last time they left. With a "See ya later," they disappeared for the time being. As for me, especially after this visit, I did what I do when I actually realize how blessed I am; I thanked God so much once more. For me, after this day, I knew a regular thanks wouldn't be nearly enough.

We Called Them Enemies

None of the visits seemed to be overly long but they were all such a blessing. They all ended with definite promises to occur again and with me thanking God "so much" that they were allowed. That was more than enough for me for now as this little glowing lady whistled her way to get me once again. Just like with my grandparents, Miss Grace seemed a bit different. She was also fully recognizable but a little more youthful in appearance. She still had those big sunglasses and that ridiculous hat on, but I could tell that something was different.

With all of the visits I was feeling a bit bolder and maybe even a little fuller of myself so I asked Miss Grace if she was feeling a little like Benjamin Button. I wanted to see her reaction, but I should have known what the answer, or lack thereof, would be because, once again, she giggled and, as usual, avoided my question. All she did was say, "Let's get a move on, Grampy," and off we went. Now there was no way that I wasn't going to talk about my visitors from that day, so, as we walked, I told her about Sammy, Sarge, my other friends and, of course, about my Nanny and Papa.

Unlike the last time where I seemed to sadden her with my words, this time she was sharing in my excitement and appreciation for the wonderful gifts that I had been given. Thinking about that, I came right out and asked her, "Where is God?" She got this huge smile on her face and stopped. She pointed at herself and at me and at everything that surrounded us and said, "God is here, he's there, he's everywhere, and he's in everything." It wasn't quite the answer that I was expecting because I didn't know any more than before I asked, but in a way, I knew what she was talking about; he is in all of us.

She went further though and said, "God is similar to that water that you believe is so holy." I didn't say anything about her ethereal eavesdropping and let her continue. She said, "Without water, nothing can live, and without God, nothing can either." Some people think they can and some people seem to for a while, but, in reality, nothing or no one ever does on their own. I don't know if I passed her secret test or if it was just time, but she told me that the destination of our journey together was a church, and, according to her, we were almost there.

I laughed a bit this time myself because, in a way, I thought this whole place was the ultimate church. In fact, I thought it was the big Kahuna of churches. She smiled and, this time, she turned the conversation away from what she just told me as if she let the cat out of the bag too early. This time, she changed our conversation back towards Sammy, Sarge, my friends and my grandparents. She spoke about them as if she loved them every bit as much as I did, and it was beautiful.

Miss Grace was on a mission herself, even though I didn't realize it at the time. Her mission was not only for me, it was every bit as much for herself as well. This time our steps seemed to be progressing towards some place closer to the light and that sweet music. Before we got all the way there though, we arrived at an old, dilapidated concrete building. This building was off the path a little ways and it blocked much of the light that I thought we were getting closer to. The building also seemed to muffle much of that beautiful music out as well. This wasn't like any church that I'd ever seen. As a matter of fact, it looked more like the bombed-out building that I was forced to stay several nights in during the war.

I almost think it was that same horrible building. I was hoping we'd walk right past it, but I should have known, we didn't. When we arrived at the steps of that so-called church, Miss Grace told me to go inside and settle in and then, as she always did, she hugged me and disappeared into all those flowers once again. As I walked through the door of the building, I noticed that she hadn't been inside prior to my arrival this time.

There was no makeshift bed made of flower petals, there was no fuzzy hammock hung between the trees, in fact, there was nothing on the floor or on the walls at all. This was that same damn cold concrete building that I prayed I never had to see again. If it wasn't the same, it was at the least an exact horrid replica. This life in between lives is so flippin' odd. I'm trying my best to see where Miss Grace is trying to take me to, but I just don't fully understand hardly anything yet, even though almost everything looks familiar in some way. As I crouched in the corner, I dropped my head towards my knees to try and rest as quickly as I could to hopefully help this day be over.

As I was lowering my head, I saw a line of men forming outside the building. Once lined up in order, they started filing into that terrible building and began making their way to me. As each man entered, they walked over to me and, one by one, each man placed their hands on my head. I was still crouched in the corner, but one came over to me and confusingly told me that they forgive me. After that, without haste, those men left out of the same door that they entered from. These men didn't have wings like Sarge or my other military buddies. They didn't have an extra glow like Miss Grace, and they weren't translucent like my grandparents.

Thank goodness they didn't have fiery eyes like Sammy originally did either. They seemed more like me than any of my other visitors did. Their skin was like mine and their other features were made of what I feel sure was their earthly characteristics like mine were. I knew there had to be a million things that I needed to be forgiven for, but I didn't have any idea why these men felt like they were the ones who had to give it.

There was exactly twelve men who riffled through that building and came over to me at first. I originally thought that, at least the pats on the head those men were giving out were a lot less painful than those of my grandfather, but, this time, there wasn't any playfulness intended by the men. This time, those pats were very serious and carried a deep meaning for all of us. As the last man came in, the thirteenth man, instead of touching my head or forgiving me as the others did, he sat down on the floor right beside me.

The man introduced himself as Nasim Amari. After our introductions were over, we just sat on the floor next to each other for a while. I guess he was trying to give me time to figure out where I'd seen him and the other men before. As politely as I could, I finally had to ask if I was supposed to know who they were. He proudly assured me that we were all a very big part of each other's lives. Although his complexion was very similar to my new one, when I really started to pay attention to him, there was no doubt that he was of Middle Eastern decent.

As I sat there thinking about where I could have possibly known these men from, it didn't occur to me to think about where it actually was, even though it should have been so obvious. I spent so much time blocking that place and those horrors out of my mind that, I guess I was still doing it then. Once I let my mind return to that hell, neither one of us had to say another word to confirm our connection. My heart sank because, although I may have not recognized them at first, I did now. here's an old saying that the eyes are the gateway to the soul, and I've seen these souls before.

There was a time where I could have sworn, I saw the souls of these men leave their bodies myself. Unfortunately, in the case of those thirteen men, it was from my own hands and the rifle that I held. This has definitely been the source of the most debilitating guilt that has completely consumed my life since the war. Mia's birth gave me the first ounce of relief since those smothering feelings began, but with Nasim sitting next to me, now offering his forgiveness, I am more sure than ever that we are more alike than most would ever admit, to include myself in my past.

Nasim confidently shook his head as to say he approved of the completion of this part of the mission. This was evidently a mission that had to happen for all of our eternal sakes, and we all had to complete it together or not at all. Before Nasim left, he asked me if he could give me a present. I already felt that I've been given more than I ever deserved, especially from those particular men, but I graciously said yes. He then asked me if I was having trouble seeing my daughter from this place. Somehow, he knew what I wanted more than I could get across to anyone else.

Not only that, he wanted to be the one to help me. What I once felt was my greatest curse is now helping me with my greatest blessing. I knew I didn't know how to tune into the living like Sammy did, but Nasim was evidentially going to show me. Nassim was probably the last person that I ever thought I'd see again and, justifiably, one that I never thought would want to help me with anything either. Although I tried my best to fight back tears, it was no use. I was getting ready to see Mia due to the great power of forgiveness.

Nasim then grabbed my hands, the very hands that were just forgiven by the thirteen men and asked me to bow my head. When he did, he smiled and simply said, "Now pray. Pray to see her." I opened one eyes wide and kind of looked up at him with my eyebrows stretched towards the sky, as to say, "Come on, man, that's it?" He laughed and said he promised that's all I had to do. That just seemed too easy and I could have done that all along if that's all it took. I told him about Sammy and all of that tuning in and the higher frequency stuff, and Nasim let out a huge laugh.

Once he gained his composure, he said, "Yeah, I have four brothers myself." After I got over the shock of the simplicity of being able to see Mia and the unheavenly feelings I was having about punching my little Herculean brother in his stupid fiery eyes, Nasim and I interlocked our hands. We then bowed our heads and prayed. This time, I kept my eyebrows down and followed Nasim's directions. As we prayed to see Mia, just as Nasim said would happen, I could finally see my baby girl.

Sammy came out of the waterfall, Sarge and my other military buddies flew from the sky. My grandparents appeared from what seemed like the ether, but where I could see Mia from made the most sense to me. Mia appeared to me from what looked like a projection that was shown directly from my heart. I could finally see my little girl. I may not be able to have quite the same interaction with her as I could with the others, but I could finally see her, and that put me at ease for a while.

My Greatest Blessing

I don't know where to begin with Mia. It was just me and her for most of her life. Although I was scared to pieces at first, as I've always said, she raised me every bit as I ever raised her, and she did well for both of us. With what I felt my curses were, I never felt that I could justify being overly religious, but no matter what feelings I may have about my own worthiness, there wasn't a day that went by that I didn't tell my little girl that I thanked God for her. She helped me become a person that I didn't think I could be anymore, and she somehow did that before she could even talk. Messing her life up in any way was never an option.

I buried all that guilt and any of the other negative feelings that I may have had as deep as I could inside of me. I kept all that death and resentment that it brought as far away from Mia as I could. I might not be with her now, but I can finally see her again, and I'll always feel that connection that I've always felt seeing her gives me an assuredness that I still need, regardless of where I am. This brings my thoughts back to an incident where I was at work and she was with the babysitter. She was running around in the house, as kids shouldn't do, but still do.

As Mia was running around, she tripped and fell, hitting the corner of her eye on a marble table. I don't know how I knew but I just felt that something was wrong with her. I called the babysitter before she had a chance to call me. I even mysteriously felt a sharp pain in my own right eye. I didn't get the seven stitches that Mia did but, to me, that connection that I already knew was there was confirmed more than ever before. That incident and so many others solidified our connection and still does to this day.

Now that I see her again, I see how sad she is without me there. I knew something was wrong, but I couldn't I couldn't see her to confirm what I already knew to be true. I was so happy to see everyone, but Mia is who I needed to see the most and I'm who I know she needs too. I don't know why I had to leave when I did. I don't think anybody ever does, but there has to be something I can do for her from here. I understand why everyone kept saying that I wasn't ready to see Mia, but when your child hurts, you hurt too, no matter where you are or what you're doing.

This place is so much like a casino. There aren't clocks or calendars around anywhere and, up until now, with all my recent visitors, I thought maybe I hit the jackpot myself, but I don't feel that way anymore. I know that Sammy, in his own playful way, was just trying to help but when it comes to Mia, I'd rather hurt than not know something's wrong with her. When Mia was really little, if she didn't have the best of days, we'd watch her favorite movie to cheer her up. That movie was Mrs. Doubtfire. There's an unwritten rule about letting a child jump on the bed, but after seeing Robin William and his children in the movie and all the fun they had, that rule simply never applied to us.

No matter where we were in the house, if we heard that song come on, Mia's eyes would light up and we'd stop whatever it was we were doing and run to the closest bed to jump on it. For me, it was like being a kid again, but for Mia, it was much more. Not only did her daddy let her break the rules, I was breaking them with her. Mia cackled and cackled watching her daddy act like a little kid jumping around with her all over the place.

We never missed an opportunity to jump either. If the song came on while we were out somewhere, instead of jumping on a bed, we'd more or less jump in place wherever we were. I think one time in Toys R US the other shoppers had to be thinking they were witnessing a dual father-daughter seizure, but we didn't care. We just did what Mr. Williams and Everlast directed us to do, we proudly jumped around. This prayer thing is simple, and in this place, it seems like we have more of a direct line to the outcome, so I'm going to try it.

As I watched Mia sadly dredging around her room, I saw her pick up some of her favorite toys and play with them for a minute or two and then put them down as if they didn't seem to be helping her with what she was feeling very much. I also heard the radio on in the background. I didn't think a prayer could be wasted on a little jumping around so that's exactly what I decided to do. I tried, I really tried, but for me alone, nothing happened. I didn't know how much time I really had so I decided to ask for help once more.

Nasim graciously obliged, and as the music started, Mia's eyes popped wide open in excitement as they always did and then, heartbreakingly, she looked around as if she was waiting for me to run in the room and start jumping with her. This was not what I intended, and when she realized that I wasn't coming, she started to cry. I know now as much as ever, when your child hurts, you hurt too, no matter where you think you are.

Green Balloons

Just before things got too sad for me to bear, Miss Grace returned. I was grateful for all Nasim's help and I let him know it as he departed. This time, she wasn't whistling or even smiling like she always did before. Her emotions seemed to mimic mine. She knew what I saw, and she also knew how I saw it too. As I left that building that I felt was one of the most terrible places I've ever been, I realized that I had a mixed opinion about it now. In one sense, I was grateful for the forgiveness that it housed, but in another, after seeing Mia like that, I resented it again.

I then turned to Miss Grace and sarcastically asked, "How could that building ever be considered a church?" Although a little more somber than usual, she still gave out another cute little giggle and said, "It's never the building, or any building for that matter, that makes a church; it's the forgiveness, love and other gifts that happen when people come together at any place that make a real church." I knew the forgiveness that I received, and at least the ability to see Mia with Nasim's help in that old concrete building, qualified that place to be as much of a church as any ever was, even though I didn't want to admit it at first.

As we walked, I realized there was no question that the path that Miss Grace led me down had deliberate resting spots along the way. Those were times for me to be still and let the plans that someone else had for me become enacted. Those times not only cleansed my soul a little at a time but also began adding clarity. They also helped me realize that Mia was still just as big of a part of my afterlife as she ever was. I refuse to ever let that go, regardless of the consequences. As we were walking, I noticed that Miss Grace appeared to be even younger than she was just the day before, and that we were getting even closer to the light and that beautiful music.

Before I could make another Benjamin Button joke, she turned to me and yelled out, "Look, look!" Her once shiny glow now turned to a more pale shade, as if she saw a ghost. The way she looked startled me for a different reason this time. I couldn't imagine what a ghost would look like in this place. I didn't know if we were in some kind of trouble or not either. As she finally gathered her words, she kept telling me to look down.

When I followed her directions, I saw all these green balloons floating through what I thought was the ground and then through the air in every direction. There were so many green balloons surrounding us in a very short amount of time that we could barely see the multitude of flowers that we usually saw and knew were there. I didn't have any idea why we were being invaded by green balloons or why they seemed to be coming from everywhere, but Miss Grace did, and she was beyond shocked to see them. To me, they were just balloons. This place was already so odd to me that a balloon didn't really shock me as it did Miss Grace.

I knew that green was my favorite color, but I didn't really have any other connection that I could think of to the balloons that were everywhere by then. Miss Grace said over and over that she'd never seen this before, "It's Mia! It's Mia, and she's doing this for you." As I, with Miss Grace's help this time, directed our prayers to see my little girl. It was her. She was releasing one green balloon after another while saying her own prayers for her daddy.

It's more than obvious to me now that prayer works in all directions, everywhere, and although I don't know if she'd ever know it or not, they were working for her too. I've been trying to signal to her, and she was doing same for me. With her much purer heart, it was working, to the amazement of Miss Grace and now to me as well. I knew that time was a little confusing here and what I thought was only a few days was obviously a few years for Mia. Unlike Miss Grace, she was aging as you're supposed to. When I looked down to see her, she must have been about ten years old or so now.

The one thing Sammy did tell the truth about was that I could see the past as well. When I looked back at Mia's past, it was a little fuzzy, but I did get to see what had been going on in her life. I saw her call my phone over and over again to hear my voice. I watched her hold onto everything that was mine as if it was me, and I also saw rivers of tears stream down her little cheeks day after day. Even though we were separated, I wasn't separated from the earthly pain of seeing her in so much pain. I had to come up with some way that I could help her.

It wasn't that she didn't have her good days, it's just that there weren't enough of them. She learned how to carry those dark clouds around with her like I used to before she was born, and it was tearing my heart to pieces. When Mia was little, obviously younger than she is now, we'd play what I called the claim game. It was a way to pass the time in the car but also a way to make the ride more enjoyable. When either of us saw a Corvette, whoever saw it first would yell out, "Claim it!" We were pretending that we'd actually own the car if we yelled out that we claimed it first.

Since there weren't a whole lot of Corvettes around where we lived, many times we'd spend a full trip just looking around in hopes of beating the other for the much-desired fictitious prize. She was so funny. When I won, she'd always come up with an excuse like she was looking at something else, or she had something in her eye. At times, she sounded like a slick city lawyer trying to defend her reasons for not winning, but other times, when she did win, she'd do her best version of a touchdown dance right underneath her tightly strapped seatbelt.

I have to admit, I did let her win sometimes just to see her seat celebration, but not all the time. Her youthful justification for not claiming a passing Corvette first was almost as comical as her seat dancing, so, either way, the game was a success to me. I know it's such a little thing, but I believe I'm going to get some help in praying for some more Corvettes and two-dollar bills to enter her life pretty soon. The two-dollar bill thing was just another game I made up too.

Because we didn't see too many of those either, I came up with a game where I told her, every time we got a two-dollar bill back as change or in a birthday card, or from anywhere, it came with one wish. This kid was so smart. On the week I came up with the game, she figured out how to cheat right away. She knew enough to ask my mother, her grandmother, to take her to the bank to get a bunch of two-dollar bills, and in doing so, she'd get all of the wishes she wanted. Once I finally got through to her that the game didn't work that way, and I laid down some ground rules, she bought into it all the way.

From there, she seemed to be satisfied with just getting the two-dollar bills and with what we called in-house wishes. I learned my lesson to be very clear with this girl because she was definitely much smarter than her father ever was. One day, she hit the proverbial jackpot herself. We were at McDonald's, her favorite restaurant, when a Corvette parked outside while we were ordering our food. She yelled out, "Claim it!" so loud that she scared the cashier. Once the worker realized that my kid wasn't robbing the place, she unknowingly gave us all two-dollar bills back for the change.

Mia got three wishes and a convertible Corvette that day. I thought she was actually going to try and kick the owner of that sleek little ride out of his own car when we left because she took that game pretty seriously at times. On this double prize day, after she finished her chicken nuggets and French fries, she told me that she made up her mind about what she wanted for her wishes. It was as if she'd been planning her desires for quite a while and just had to wait for the arrival of the next two-dollar bill before it could come true.

Once the next one or three on this day made their way to her, she looked up at me with those big, brown puppy dog eyes and said, "Daddy, my wish is for us to be together forever." Now, I don't care how big and tough any father thinks he is, those words from your little girl are pretty special. Her wish was so special to me that I was pretending that I had something in my eye so she wouldn't see me proudly choking up. I know I couldn't help it, or even do anything about it, but I do feel, to a degree, that I broke my promise to her. She knows I didn't want to get sick and she has to know I didn't want to leave her. It wasn't my decision. It wasn't my choice either. I could barely stand there and watch her hurt for me like all those green balloons were telling me she still was.

Her Mama, Mia And My Parents

I wasn't married to Emily, Mia's mother, very long. After Mia was born, she said she had some things to work out, and I knew she did, so she left both of us for quite a while. She came back a few years later and I honestly do think she ended up finding whatever it was she was looking for. At first, I was mad. I was hurt, but most of all, I was scared about how someone like me could ever raise a little girl on my own. I had just gotten out of the military and I was still full of all that death. I was still freshly fighting with my own demons at the time. Once I realized I was all that little girl had, failure, for any reason, was never an option.

My original circumstances as a father was kind of like the first time that we entered the actual war zone. It had to be all in or not at all and doing nothing never crossed my mind when it came to her. I've had massive issues with guilt before, and much of that was released to a great degree by Nasim and his men in that old concrete building, but I would have never been able to live with the guilt that not giving Mia my best would have brought. I know my thoughts are so dramatic at times but so was my life.

For some reason, my low times seemed to always involve someone dying, which, to me, was the lowest of the lows. My highs, however, included growing up with an amazing family and having some of the truest friends a man could have. The kind that would literally lay their own life down for you. My greatest high of highs, however, was not only having Mia, but the fact that it was just us for so long. I think if the situation at her birth with her mother would have been any different than it was, I may have never realized, out of my own ignorance or selfishness, how much of a blessing she actually was.

That little girl came to me at my most vulnerable time and needed me to be the best me I could be. My issues could have only hurt her, so I hid them. I don't care if I would have found the cure for cancer or discovered a new continent, there is no greater accomplishment that could have been more satisfying than living out my role as her father, even for the limited time I was able to. There were times that I doubted my ability to give her what I thought she deserved but, for once, I didn't dwell on what I wasn't, I just moved forward to what I could be, and it seemed to work out for both of us.

By the time Emily really returned to Mia's life, it wasn't too long after that I became sick. Sickness was like everything else my life. I didn't play around with it and it took me to this place in a hurry. I didn't tell anyone about my health issues, mainly because of how fast it developed and swallowed me up. I was glad Emily did what she had to do, when she did, because it seemed to be just in time. If I have any consolation in having to leave, it's to see that Mia's mother is finally the mother that both of them need her to be. They don't have to have the relationship that Mia and I did because they have they their own now.

That's the way it's supposed to be. Just like Mia did with me, she's raising her mom well. Another consolation that I have is that Mia gets to spend a lot of time with my parents. My parents lost two children and, regardless of our ages, I don't think there's much worse of a thing for a parent to have to live through. Seeing them spend time with Mia fills my heart and, believe me, as grandparents, they are way more patient than they ever were with their own boys.

Of course, a little girl is much different than three bone-headed boys who fought all the time, but still, they've changed. My mother, who was so quick to pull a belt out on us—or should I say, on me—now sits on the floor and does crafts and art projects with my little girl. She's now so calm and peaceful. I jokingly ask myself if this is even the same lady. The funniest thing is that my once macho dad has given away all his testosterone.

He now has tea parties and lets Mia do his hair and fingernails. What in the world did she do to him? I guess love for that little thing has taken all his masculinity away, but I get it. I know Mia and Jacob's kids have helped them get through some things that no parent should ever have to go through. I'm still going to punch Sammy when I see him, though, for telling me all that bull about tuning in. I should have known, when love's involved, all you ever have to do is pray and be thankful. Looking at my parents, I'm definitely grateful for them. They sacrificed so much for us and, unlike now, I'm sure we didn't show the appreciation at the time that they deserved, even though all of us truly always felt it.

M. A. COLE

Uncomfortably Numb

Slowly but surely and somewhat intermittently, my own prayers began to work. The issue was, what seemed like only a few days for me was obviously many more for those I prayed to see, if I could see them at all. Their lives appeared to be on a fast forward setting while my life here was in super slow motion. There were so many things I thought I'd be able to see, even if it had to be from afar. I can remember after my grandparents died, I hoped, even prayed myself, that they weren't watching down on me. Mainly because I never wanted them to see the many things that I felt I was forced to do, but also because of just as many things I chose to do on my own.

I wasn't very proud of myself for many reasons back then and I just figured they wouldn't be very proud of me either. I just didn't want to miss anything myself, but it seems like I've missed a lot. Mia has grown up and changed so much now. She's a beautiful young woman now and I think she's even beginning to drive. To me, she doesn't look like she has that overwhelming sadness anymore, thank God, but she is still kind of to herself and more of a recluse than I ever hoped she would be.

She seems to have more of a select group of friends, and, other than being around them for a while at times, she seems to be by herself a great deal. I am glad I was right about her mom. She's playing the role of the mother and father, and probably every bit as well as I ever did, or at least tried to. I didn't think that there were supposed to be any sad feeling in a place like this but, considering what I've been through so far and now looking down at my daughter, being here leaves me with an emptiness more so than anything else.

It's definitely not like anything I was ever told or expected it to be like. I missed so much of Mia's life, even from a distance. I still believe being able to see her is better than not being able to, but just like when Miss Grace asked me if felt I had an unfinished life, how could I still feel any other way? I'm so used to things not being like I thought they would be; it's kind of making me a little numb to this whole death and great beyond thing. Numbness is something I mastered over the years and I guess I'll perfect it here.

Every time someone else died in my life, at first there came that excruciating pain. If something didn't come in to relieve that initial agony, I believe, in many cases, I would have died long before I actually did. It was that numbness that always came in to mask the pain. It wasn't necessarily a welcomed guest, but it was one that allowed me to press on with whatever it was I had to do to survive. I know I should be more grateful that I'm not fighting real demons with their own fiery eyes at that other place because I do get to see so many of my loved ones from here, but my child's happiness trumps all that for me.

My problem is twofold. On one hand, it seems I really can't seem to help or even do anything but see Mia every now and then, but on the other, I won't allow myself to fully feel the great blessings that this place has already given me. My Papa said that free will was created here, and I believe him, but my freedom doesn't feel so free. I can't go where I want or do what I want, and I'm on some guided path to God-knows-where. In order to have free will, I thought you at least get to have some of your own choices, but I don't. I have the unwelcomed guest of numbness instead.

This time, instead of Miss Grace coming to get me, it was Sammy. I knew I owed him a punch in the nose for not explaining this tuning in or prayer thing better, but I also knew I'd never do it. He was flexing all his parts up and down just as much as he did the other day, and we both were just as happy to each other again we he came over to me too. Even with me, there are times that I do allow myself to brush that dark cloud aside. Sammy told me Miss Grace would be busy for a while and that I'd see her later. I asked him jokingly if she had a fingernail appointment or had to get her hair done, or something like that because I didn't know what could possibly be more important than taking me to wherever it was, we were going. Sammy must have learned a thing or two from Miss Grace because he basically ignored my comments and we did what we always do when we were together. We joked around and thought about ways to mess stuff up.

Uncle Trickery

Almost as soon as Sammy put his mind to it, he told me what he came up with. He told me he wanted to play a trick on Mia's boyfriend. "Boyfriend?" I said. I haven't been able to see her much at all from here and I damn sure didn't see or know about any boyfriend. I didn't even get a chance to interrogate whoever this little punk was, but now, I'm all in for Sammy's plan. "Let's go boyfriend hunting," I said back to Sammy rather quickly. To me, in my mind, Mia was still that little girl. I don't want to hear about any boyfriend. Once that boy came in sight, I shook my head while Sammy hardily laughed at my expense.

This kid had one of those stubby, dog-tail-looking things on the back of his head. I was ex-military and definitely from a different era. I had no idea what Mia could see in a guy with some man bun thing sprouting out. I also figured out in a short amount of time that his name was Wayne. Immediately, I started to rant. "Who the hell names their kid Wayne?" This kid was definitely not John Wayne or Wayne Gretzky, and if I have anything to do with it, it'll never be Wayne's World either.

To me, he was more like Wayne, Wayne go away and don't come back another day. That's it. The microphone has dropped. My girl was just a baby last week. *Oh no*, I thought. I may have been sad before at times but, even from here, I'm getting kind of worked up and Sammy can't stop egging it on. I know that jerk is loving this too because, once again, he's getting me and that kid at the same time. "W-A-Y-N-E," I said in my slowest whiny voice.

He seemed so damn awkward that it was almost a shame to do something to him, but hey, if Sammy said it was a good idea, who was I to argue him? I was the rookie here. I was still pretty new at what I could do or couldn't do from this place so, once again, I had to rely on my brother—the same one that I should have tuned into punching, but he was the only option that I had. Again, with time being somewhat funny, we could tell that the poochy-headed kid was getting ready for some kind of fancy event like a prom or homecoming. As Sammy and I watched him brush his stub several times, I said, "How hard would it be to blow up his house from here?" I was just joking about that, I think, but what we decided to do was almost as detrimental to that young man's plans for the evening.

When Sammy was alive, everyone he met instantly loved him. That meant everywhere. Without exaggeration, he was just that type of person. I'm glad for us now that every animal did too. I'm pretty sure that, with his current higher influence, they still will too. I think the plan was set without the real need of working out any overly-specific details. Animals, especially dogs, have a keen sense and are very good, in most cases, at following directions. We watched for a little while longer until W-A-Y-N-E finished primping, as little girls do, and left his house.

Then he headed to Emily and Mia's house to where I was hoping all the festivities would begin. This boy was driving a huge Toyota truck with massive tires and the most obnoxious horn ever installed. I thought, *daddys not being around really does make a difference in a daughter's life* after seeing this bonehead. As the funny-named kid arrived to pick up Mia, he leaned over in the seat, looked at himself in the mirror and sprayed some kind of spray in his mouth, I guess to disinfect his breath, but if it's up to me, his breath isn't going to be anywhere near Mia.

Anyway, I don't think Sammy ever stopped laughing as he mysteriously contacted one of his earthly friends. This friend was something I guess you could call a dog and one that was just a few yards away from the front steps that W-A-Y-N-E had to go up to get Mia. Sammy has always been over the top, and this prank was no different. He could have picked a Beagle; he could have even picked a Labrador Retriever. They're common dogs in the K-9 world, but not for Sammy. As Wayne rang the doorbell, Mia and Emily came out on the front porch. Mia was beautiful and so grown-up-looking.

She had this long, flowing, purple dress on and she looked almost exactly like her mother did when I first met her. She was almost grown and, finally, she seemed so happy...even if it was with W-A-Y-N-E. I almost forgot Sammy and I were on a mission, but he didn't. After that boy reached in to give Mia a hug, everyone on the porch jerked their heads around in a hurry to see what was approaching with such a clatter. It was as if they heard a train coming their way, but this train had slobber slapping out of both sides of its mouth. I think if Sammy could have used a dinosaur, he would have, but what he did use was pretty close.

As the porch dwellers started shuffling, Sammy's new buddy, a humongous St. Bernard, was headed their way. I say their way, but he was most definitely directed solely at W-A-Y-N-E. Before that mammoth dog made it all the way to the porch, I confirmed with Sammy that his new friend, Cujo, wasn't actually going to kill the kid. Without giving me a clear answer, once again, Sammy laughed and just told me to watch. That dog acted like Wayne had a prime rib in his pocket and sloppily bit down right around his crotch area. I don't like cussing here, but even I had to say, "D-A-M-N."

The dog wasn't hurting him or his body parts, but it sure did a number on his finely-pressed yuppie pants as they ripped off so easily, leaving him completely in his underwear and, more importantly, running back to his swamp buggy to head back to where he came. That kid screamed louder than his obnoxious horn could blow. Mia and Emily tried not to laugh, but it was funny. There was ample laughter from above and below.

After they went back in the house and Wayne made it back to his own house again, we could tell that the boy was still embarrassed, and when he tried round two at getting ready for the dance, he began talking to himself in the mirror. His words were mostly about that big, old, stupid dog, as he described Sammy's new pet. He also fussed about how that thing all but molested him right there in Mia's front yard. We were laughing at the kid's commentary almost as much as we did about the attack. The thing is, after a while of listening to his blubbering, I could tell this kid really liked Mia.

I don't care if I was there or here, I had to check any boy out who was going to be around my daughter. Sammy finally caught his breathe from all the laughter and let me know that was one of his favorite pranks of all time. I had to agree, but I really wanted to know more about this boy and more about how Sammy actually got the dog to do that. I wanted to be able to interact with her too if I felt I needed to, even if that help had to be delivered through some huge, horse-looking dog.

A Different Opinion

After that kid primped once again, he jumped back in that over-sized truck and headed back to try and pick up Mia for the second time. Sammy asked me if we should start planning the second round, but something inside me felt like he had enough for one day. This time, when he went to the door he was as nervous as I've ever seen anyone wearing a man bun, but that's understandable, I guess. I did have Sammy make sure that big St. Bernard was on standby just in case. When Mia opened the door, they both laughed, and he politely walked her down the steps, making sure her dress didn't drag on the ground.

He was definitely looking all around for a certain four-legged friend and he was definitely pulling at his pants to make sure they stayed on this time, but most of his attention was where I thought it should be. He even opened the truck door for Mia and gave her a boost up into that ridiculous thing. He may have known I was watching from somewhere because he even watched the placement of his hands while helping her in too. This kid at least scored one point with me and he's definitely not a quitter.

When I was his age, if a massive dog tried to bite my parts and pants off, I would have definitely seen that as a sign to stay away, but not him. I wondered at first, mainly because Sammy was whispering doubts in my ear about if this guy was as genuine as he seemed to be. Watching them at that dance was truly heart-warming. He never stopped being polite and he did seem to be real. As they sat down to drink what I hoped was a non-alcoholic refreshment, I listened in, as everyone seems to always do to me. They were still talking about the front porch assault but they both spoke about their fathers. Wayne spoke of his and Mia about me.

Although I didn't know Wayne's father and hadn't met him here yet either, he was one of the young men who didn't make it home from the same war I was in. I thought to myself, *dammit, now I have to like this kid*. The more he and Mia spoke, the more I actually did like him. Sammy didn't catch on yet; he was playing the air violin in the background and still flexing. As the night went on, I realized that Mia was almost a woman and this guy was almost a man himself.

The respect that he showed my daughter turned any anxiety that I may have had into appreciation for him. By the end of the night, even Uncle Trickery liked the guy too. Sammy did have a funny nickname for Wayne, though, and I also thought it would stick if nowhere else but here. Sammy's silly self gave the boy the nickname of WEE-WEE W-A-Y-N-E and he laughingly kept saying over and over again. I guess you never really know anyone's story until you stop and listen, or at least, eavesdrop if you can. As Wayne dropped Mia off, he was just as cordial, and helped her out of his truck and back to the house.

They hugged and kissed each other on the cheek, but that was it. *I might be able to handle these Hallmark moment kinds of dates,* I thought. He did still look in every direction when he headed back to his truck, but this kid really was a good guy, and I was proud of him and the way he handled himself with my daughter, even though he'd probably never know it. When Mia went inside, she excitedly told her mother about her night and how much fun she had. This was the happiness that I always prayed she'd have. I was kind of hoping I was the one that caused it, but Mia's okay and this kid is too.

Emily then told Mia about the first time we met, which was very different, and in a bar, but she left out those kind of details as she told our story. She said she can see herself in Mia. I thought to myself, *slow it down, now,* but I understood what she was saying. Emily was very happy when we first met but she had family problems that ended up consuming her and our marriage. I got Mia in the process of her mom trying to find her way back from her past, and that gift was my greatest by far.

Emily's a wonderful mother and Mia seems like she's as happy as any teenager can be. She does seem very mature for her age and, with the exception of his hair, so does Wayne. I guess losing a father makes you grow up faster than what seems fair, but these kids are going to be just fine. Now that we've finished playing tricks on people, I'm not going to let Sammy go anywhere until he helps me become a little more like Houdini myself.

Houdini

Even though Sammy plays a lot, he knows when I'm serious about something. At least now I'm somewhat at ease about how Mia is doing. So now I want his help for more positive reasons than I probably would have ever wanted it for before now. I understand that prayer and belief is key, but I couldn't pray that dog into biting that boy in the crotch when Sammy could. I want to know what he knows, and this time, I'm not going to let him leave until he shows me. When I asked Sammy to teach me all his mystical ways, he laughed and said, "Did Houdini tell his secrets?"

I don't know about what Houdini did or didn't do, but I knew who I was going to make spill the beans before they could leave. Like I've been thinking and even saying since I got to this place, it's still so much like home and, for whatever reason, I'm still the big brother in this situation. Sammy never cared before about telling me any secrets; in fact, he was the worst secret keeper there ever was, and this time was no different. It's not that any of it was ever a secret at all anyway; it was more of a process. I simply had to take it in a little at a time.

Maybe everyone who said it was right. Maybe before now I wasn't ready, but now I'm kind of accepting where I am. I just want to be able to do more while I'm here; more for me, but, more importantly, more for Mia. In truth, I even understand the life in between lives thing to a degree. With almost everything, to include a meal, there has to be a cleansing and preparation stage to lead off the main course. Those forced naps that Miss Grace made me take, my visits that I was so blessed to receive, and even what seemed like a never-ending path, all have a purpose. That purpose was to prepare me for whatever is at my own final destination.

There's no question that we have a say in how that is constructed. Look at Sammy, Sarge and my buddies, and even my grandparents. They all came to me in a way that, after I thought about it for a while, I could somewhat understand. Even the way Mia projected out of my own heart made more sense to me now more than ever. I knew I wasn't ready to be completely engulfed in that light, but hopefully I'm more ready than I was.

Nasim and his men really helped me take leaps and bounds towards that direction and I'm grateful for it. I don't know If I could have handled that when I first arrived here. Believe it or not, that kid with the man bun, seeing Emily as she was and seeing Mia so happy also helped so much. From the moment I got here, most of my thoughts were on Mia and her sadness. Most of my thoughts are still on Mia, but there's a relaxation in my heart now. She's mostly grown and seems to be having a pretty good life, whether I'm there or not; that's all I ever wanted.

I guess this is that letting go that people talk about. The harder we seem to fight against something, the more it seems to persist or resist what we're trying to do. My life was such a battle at times that I seemed to still have some of that resistance in me here. I think that's why it was so hard for me to see Mia at times, or also the reason I couldn't be the one who befriended that huge St. Bernard. Sammy just prayed it into existence without a second thought about that dog not ripping W-A-Y-N-E's pant off.

He knew it was going to happen because he was clear on what he was asking for, and, although it appeared to be a malicious act, it really wasn't. That boy had to go through that too for me to be able to see that he really was a good guy. I don't know if Sammy was actually praying for that to happen or for me to be able to see the truth, but, either way, it worked. Maybe none of this is as hard as I'm making it after all. This rambling was a conversation that I was trying to have with Sammy, but after I finished, he said, "See, now you're Houdini too." My eyebrow wanted to come up again as it did when Nasim told me all I had to do was pray to see Mia.

Of course, this was after Sammy misguided me with all that tuning in mess, but maybe, just maybe they were both right. I guess another way of putting it is, letting go is actually the same thing as having faith, and tuning in has to be the same as cleansing and preparing yourself for the request. I told Sammy this life in between life thing is pretty deep. He smiled at me and said, "Naw, only as deep as you make it."

I wanted to confirm that I had everything straight, so I said, "You mean, all you have to do is prepare yourself for the prayer, pray, have faith that your prayer will be answered, and to top it all off, you give thanks for when it is?" Sammy said, while half- heartedly listening to my description, "Yep, that's it." I was expecting a little more expansion on the subject, but I didn't get it. He just kept calling me Houdini and flexing his muscles, thinking about something else for us to get into. He did mumble something about there being one more little thing, but it wasn't a big deal.

I had this thought before but, at that point, I really began to notice that, even though Sammy looked like a man on the outside, he was really still that same little boy I grew up with on the inside. I guess here, once you learn how, you can look like whatever you want to. Regardless of what his outside appearance was, his beautiful insides were very much the same. He was fifteen years old and I'd be willing to bet that, somewhere underneath that masculine puffiness, he still is now.

His innocence gave him the preparation. His loving heart gave him the faith. Our wonderful parents taught him how to pray, and his light-hearted view on life gave him his assuredness. I think he was trying to hide it, but when he got ready to leave that day, instead of him telling me a secret, I told him how proud I was of him. Not the puffy, in-shape parts, but the part inside that made him Sammy. I looked at Sammy and thanked him. He smacked me on the arm and said, "We can play pranks on anyone you want, just let me know." I said, "No, not for the pranks, even though that St. Bernard thing was funny." "Well, for what?" he asked. I said, "For being my brother, no matter where we are."

This Brutus-looking man got the good type of tears in his eyes. The kind that fifteen-year-olds so easily do, but this time, instead of flexing anything up and down, he appeared to me as he was on earth, Down Syndrome and all, and gave me a hug every bit as strong as his muscled-up self ever could. He taught me so much in life, and now he has here as well without even really trying. As he walked off, all I heard was Houdini...Houdini... but, once again, all I could do was thank God so much for so many things but today, a little extra for my sweet brother.

Cerulean Blue

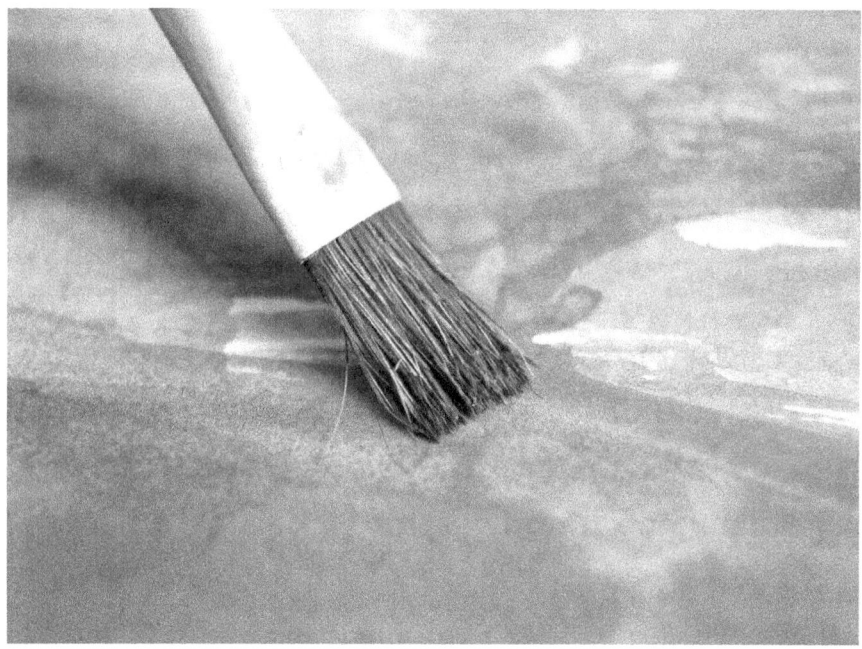

Miss Grace seemed to be slacking in her tour guide duties because I hadn't seen her in a while and I kind of missed that sweet old lady. I jokingly thought to myself, *I guess she must have gotten held up in St. Michael's hair cuttery or maybe at Abraham's antiques*. I had no clue where she was but, for the first time since I've been here, I was going to have to find my own resting place. I didn't realize it at first, but I almost got to where I looked forward to those little breaks. I was never really tired, but ,to me, it seemed that each resting spot brought something that always seemed to get me a little closer to that light and music, and to whatever my final destination is.

If Miss Grace was here, I would ask her about my theory, but she's not, so I'm going to have to try and figure it out for myself. I was fairly sure that any place I chose would be considered safe in this neighborhood, so off I went. I wasn't looking for any particular place, but like everything and everyone else here, it found me. Before Sammy died, we were in a boating accident that hurt him pretty badly. He already had so many health problems towards the end that I felt I added to his problems.

Instead of sticking around to help out, I went to Israel on a study abroad program for the summer. A whole lot happened in that country, but one of the biggest things I did was paint something that I couldn't take the credit for at all. Don't get me wrong, it was my hand and my time, and I was actually the one who put the paint on the canvas, but that was about it. It was like every idea and image flowed to me completely from somewhere else so effortlessly. When I was finished, I had never seen anything like what that painting was.

Its features were just as special as Miss Grace's eyes or even her glow, but different. It was almost as pure as our skin is now but with many colors perfectly blended around the other, rather than in one unified shade. When I started painting, I didn't stop until what I can only call the channeled masterpiece was finished. After Sammy died, I didn't paint anymore and, out of rage from the loss of my brother, I destroyed something that wasn't mine to ruin. It wasn't too long after that I joined the military.

When Mia was small, I bought her little art sets and, although we did have fun with them, we did no more than doodle out cartoons. I started painting to teach Sammy how to do it for himself and, without him, I didn't think it was fair for me to continue. I don't feel that way anymore. I see how well he's doing, and I also see a full-fledged art set sitting in the middle of the woods. Miss Grace isn't fooling me. She may be pre-occupied, but not busy enough not to give me another much-needed gift. Just like so many years ago, once I started painting, I couldn't stop.

I don't know how long I actually painted that night, but I do know I only stopped when no more paint fit anywhere on the canvas. The result this time was every bit as magical as the first, if not more. I've learned that I shouldn't expect anything else from a place like this, so I won't. Once again, I really couldn't take credit for this one either, but it didn't matter. I had that old feeling of true accomplishment that I hadn't had in such a long time. I can remember the last painting and even the color that most often permeated throughout what I felt I had inherited.

It was Cerulean Blue. That shade of blue is a little like a deep sky blue, or maybe even the color of a clear sea, the kind you can see all the way to the bottom of. It was mesmerizing then and even more so now. I didn't want to stop painting, but it was time. I finished all I was given to do. To me, this day was a glaring metaphor for my life. Many times, it was messy, similar to paint that I spilled all over the forest floor, but other times it produced something far greater than I could have ever imagined.

Both Mia and those paintings were so much better than anything I could have ever produced on my own. So, without hesitation, once again, I thanked God so much, but this time, it wasn't just for the outcome. For the first time ever, it was also for the spilled paint of my life as well. All the good and the bad has made this, and how amazing it is, and I'm finally realizing that.

Abby For Short

L ife was so funny at times, but death is so odd as well. There is really very little difference so far between the two. Before here, I woke up, went to work, spent time with my family, went back to sleep, sometimes had dreams, and sometimes didn't. I can't see how this place has been that much different. Seeing Mia with a boy, polite or not, didn't ease my mind. Seeing the contentment that Mia learned how to create in herself did.

The fact that I feel she's going to be alright now put me in a different frame of mind. I still wish I could have seen the years that I missed or even been able to help her in some way, but they went by too fast, and when I tried to "tune" into that part of her life, it was simply too fuzzy. No matter what happened, she's happy, so I'm happy too. That bond between us definitely began when even my stubbornness realized there was such preciousness in her mother's womb, and it hasn't left. My life nor hers was one that most would consider easy, but she mastered her challenges much better than I did.

As I did when I was young, and not having Miss Grace to direct me any differently, I laid on my back again and just looked up at those magnificent clouds. Not one of those puffy canvases in their own right contained even the slightest ounce of darkness. Lying there, I looked over at my painting that I had propped up next to a tree every now and then, and when I did, the clouds, the sky, and even the painting itself seemed to become even brighter than it originally was. I felt like I was that same kid of my youth. That kid didn't realize he'd ever have a worry in the world and, right then, neither did I.

I have known pain and I've seen so much death, but I've also seen where all ends up—here. If the destination is better than this place right now, I can't even imagine how glorious it will be. Finally, I hear the leaves rustling, *I'm going to get on Miss Grace for abandoning me*, I jokingly thought. It wasn't Miss Grace coming this time, though. It wasn't Sammy or Sarge, or Nasim either. It was a little, brown-headed girl. I knew it wasn't Mia, but she looked very much like her around the time of my death.

Just like Miss Grace always did, this little girl came up to me as if she had known me forever and said, "Hey, Grampy." This kid was just as sassy and funny as Miss Grace was, but in a miniature, much faster version. She noticed my painting and ran over to it. I didn't have a house here, and I'm guessing I'm what you'd call a transient, so, when she asked me if she could borrow it, I didn't see any issue with her request. Besides, I remembered it wasn't really mine anyway. She looked deep into that painting for a while like she knew what every brush stroke meant and what they meant to me too.

I could tell she appreciated the painting and I thought about asking her if she wanted to paint something together, but I'd already spilled most of the paint that I didn't use and there really wasn't any to speak of left. She didn't have time to paint anyway because she told me that we had to get a move on. We had a lot to do, and we didn't have a lot of time to do it either. This little girl cracked me up. I guess she thought she was Miss Grace's personal secretary or some other sort of important confidant.

Just like when I wasn't bold enough to refuse the orders from my glowing elderly chaperone, I didn't have guts to deny the directions from a sassy little girl either. I rapidly followed her directions and went to grab my painting to take it along with us. I didn't mind if she borrowed it or even kept it. I figured, by now, I'd be able to paint another one anytime I wanted to, but she wasn't having any of that. She wanted to carry it herself. The painting was almost as big as she was and, as we made our way back to the path, she'd peak over and around the edges of the canvas every now and then to make sure she didn't run into anything.

I asked her where Miss Grace was and if she even knew her. I've learned there's no guessing about anything in this place. She told me she was close, and she's always been with me, and always will. I've heard those words before but obviously their definition of being around and mine are very different. As strange as it sounds, and being that Miss Grace seemed to be aging in reverse, a weird thought came over me in this odd place, so I asked, "Are you Miss Grace?" I got a very similar reaction that Miss Grace gave when I asked if she was God.

The Missing Years

That little girl laughed while shaking her head and said, "My name is Abigail, Abby for short." Now, this still didn't tell me where Miss Grace was or why this little girl was now my very active chauffer, but she evidently was and, per her demand, off we went. I guess carrying around that painting finally got a little awkward for Abby because she told me she'd be back in a minute and disappeared through the flowers that inhabited everywhere. She came back in just a few minutes, as she said she would, without it. She assured me that she just put it in safe keeping for now and we had to keep moving. Now, Mia could be strong-willed when she wanted to be, but this little girl, Abby, she was definitely bold to say the least.

She was so cute and confident that I really didn't have any other choice but to do what she asked, but still. On the path, this time I could tell we were getting extremely close to where I'm guessing was the end of it, which was the destination, I'm assuming. As we walked, it was refreshing to be around a little girl again. She, unlike Miss Grace, went on and on about any and everything that she saw and thought she saw.

She had such amazement with everything. Her age and above was the part of Mia's life that I missed. It was so peculiar how comfortable we were around each other once I got used to her confidence. There wasn't an ounce of shyness about her, just a curiosity about everything, to include me, and I had the same interest in her. She was the first child that I'd seen since I've been here and, thinking about Sammy, I wondered if she chose to look that way or if someone chose for her. I didn't know how to ask a little girl that question, so I decided to leave it as a mystery.

Abby asked me if I knew what her name meant. I had a blank stare on my face because I really didn't know what my own name meant, and my name was Israel, so I felt I should at least know that. I said, "Why don't you tell me?" I said that so I wouldn't sound as ignorant as I was to the question. She gave this big grin and said, "Abigail means the bringer of joy." I smiled back because, as happy and energetic as this kid was, I could definitely see that. She'd walk for a bit, then almost jog with a skip thrown in every now and then.

I may have never been tired before but keeping up with Abby was a job. If I'd fall a little behind, she'd look back and say, "Pick it up, Grampy," and I'd do my best to catch up with her as quickly as I could. I even tried to make up conversations so she'd slow down a bit, but she kept up with the conversation much better than I did with her pace. I could tell that she felt we had to be somewhere at a specific time, but I didn't know why. This was the first time that time itself seemed to be a factor. Besides, there was no way for me to be late for my own funeral because that already happened.

After a while, as kids her age do, and all at once, she seemed to get tired, really tired, as if she wore her own self out. I asked her if she wanted to take a break, but she said we couldn't and asked if she could ride on my back. At this point, I felt I was ready to fall out too but, without hesitation, I kind of felt like it was an honor that she even asked. I missed things like this with my own daughter, so I proudly scooped her up and spun her to my back. She didn't feel like she weighed much more than a feather, so it wasn't that difficult to keep on the path at pretty much the same speed she was fussing about me going earlier.

I walked for maybe ten steps and her little head rested on my left shoulder and, shortly thereafter, she was asleep. I forgot how quick kids at this age crash. It's sixty to zero in three point three seconds sometimes. I decided to keep walking in the direction we were headed just in case she woke up. I didn't want that little girl fussing at me again. Like everything else that has happened in this place, I'm sure whatever it is we're supposed to see will find us long before I even know that I'm looking for it anyway. I think Abby was dreaming as she napped on my shoulder because, every now and then, I'd hear a faint little murmur.

It was so cute. This walk just felt so fatherly. This was the kind of thing I missed so much that I wasn't sure I wanted to her to wake up for a while. She slept on my back for about thirty minutes and, just like when you put a car battery on a charger, she woke up as energized as ever. She may have been a little embarrassed about falling asleep but, when she climbed down, she didn't walk quite as far in front of me this time, even though she definitely talked as much as she had before. I didn't mind it, though. It was cute, and she was so animated.

Listening to her was the most true personal excitement that I've had since I've been here. When she gave me a chance to get a word in, I asked her why she and Miss Grace always called me Grampy. She laughed as if it was some state secret and basically did what Miss Grace always did. She completely ignored my question and kept talking about whatever it was she wanted to talk about. That little bugger was outsmarting me too. I figured maybe I could outsmart some answers out of her myself, but it didn't work. When I asked where Miss Grace was again, Abby scrunched up her little nose and said, "She told she'd always be with you and always would be with you, man."

Her answer didn't "answer" anything at all and I thought this little thing might need a time out. When I thought about those words, "time out," I immediately thought back to Mia and the one and only time out she was ever sentenced to. I can't say that Mia was ever that bad. I never had to spank her, not that I could anyway. In many ways my kid made me a wuss, but I did have to put her in time out one time.

It was only once, but you would have thought I sentenced her to thirty years of hard time. I really don't think she understood what was going on, but I had to do something so she wouldn't see me vent and then laugh at her attempt to get her point across. One afternoon, I was fixing dinner and she was playing in her room. All of a sudden, I heard this terrible pounding coming from the back of the house. I ran back there as fast as I could to see what was going on. When I saw what my child had done, Tim The Tool Man may have been proud of her, but I was a little upset to say the least.

Mia evidentially saw me cooking hamburgers for dinner. She never had any problem with eating hamburgers before, and I thought she liked them, so I was making that meal again. *Hamburgers and macaroni and cheese; that's a good meal for anyone*, I thought. When I looked around this little girl's room, it didn't take but a second to realize that she nailed two hand-drawn pictures of a cow with a red x through it on her wall. I don't know what she was thinking.

I didn't know what to say. I didn't know that she knew where my hammer and nails were or that she even really knew how to use them correctly, but she obviously did. I didn't even know that she knew hamburgers were made from cows. I was absolutely speechless, and she was overly-proud of herself, I thought. I still don't know how, at her age, she knew what putting a red x across something really meant but, to her, I soon learned that it meant eat more chicken. I didn't know if I should laugh, get the putty, or really what to do or what was going on. I did know that my little protester evidently was watching way too much television, and most definitely too many of those dumb Chic-Fil-A commercials, and for that, her one and only time out soon followed.

The Elders

Thinking back to Mia and my mother sitting on the floor playing and doing little art projects together so peacefully, I fully understood that times had changed, and changed a lot. If Jacob, Sammy, or I did what Mia did with the cow nailed to the wall thing, my mother, Quick Draw McGraw, would have definitely handled the situation a bit differently. In her defense, though, we did so much wrong most of the time, we left her very few other choices.

Walking and talking with Abby has been so enjoyable. She has many of the same mannerisms that Mia did, but also the boldness and confidence of Miss Grace. This little thing is a mess as she's kicking at my feet while I walk. Before long, she smiled again and said, "We're here." I looked around and said, "We're where?" The beautiful music was louder, but we weren't all the way to the light yet, so I don't know what "here" she's talking about. Besides, I thought it was Miss Grace's job to get me to the destination or the light, or wherever it was I was supposed to end up at.

Abby grabbed me by the hand and led me over a small hill that was hiding the "we're here" she was talking about. When we reached the top of the hill, there was a hundred or more people just about twenty yards or so away. As we reached the middle of that crowd, Abby seemed to be showing me off like I was a new doll baby or the shiniest penny in a shiny penny contest. Before I could introduce myself by my real name, Israel, she'd beat me to the punch and introduce me as Grampy. It was like a whirlwind meeting one person after another until we got around to just about everyone.

The gathering reminded me of one of those country family reunions where you know you're related to everyone there, but you don't really know most of them. This place was no different because I realized I did know at least some of these people from the past. I saw my great uncle and a few older cousins. I saw other kids there too. I even saw one of my neighbors who, like me, had no idea how he could end up in such an oddly wonderful place. I thought maybe this was the destination or at least the check-in line of it.

I didn't think those thoughts long though because neither Miss Grace, my grandparents, Sammy, Sarge or any of the other people were there. If this Rain in the sky ever makes it that far, I know, without a shadow of a doubt, they'll all be the first ones in line letting out a sigh of relief. Since Sammy wants to be roommates again—God, I pray that's not possible—he'd probably be at the front of the group with a sublease in his hand. No, this gathering looked more like a giant pizza party without the pizza. There was just fellowship and laughter.

The kids, to include Mia, were running around playing so I can see if the others were here this would be more like what I'd expect an arrival such as this to be. The one thing I did notice was that there was a long table where the most elderly people were sitting. This place never ceases to amaze me. The similarities to an actual family reunion kept piling up. When Abby took a break from playing with the other children, she once again grabbed me by the hand and led me over to the elders.

Now, I didn't recognize any of these people at all but, even though I still wasn't sure if you could live in any form after you reached the destination, I didn't understand why they'd stay old. Once again, Abby introduced me as Grampy, and, this time, she was doing it to a few that fit the bill plus some. As they greeted me back, they told me who they were in relation to me. Some of those men and women went back four or more generations and they, like everyone was since I got to this place, were so glad to see me.

We all visited for a while and Abby, once again, told me we had to get a move on. I guess the party was over because when Abby said we had to do something, it didn't take too long before we were doing it. As we got to the other side of that hill, I saw something that was a first for me in this place. It was an animal. In fact, it was dog, and not just any dog either; it was our old dog Puddles and he was way happier to see me than any of the people I rekindled with here were.

Puddles

I think if people knew how to love the way that dogs do, the world would be a much better place. Puddles was actually Sammy's dog, but he was equally Jacob's and mine as well because we were all always together. I had an old Jon boat growing up and I always heard having a boat without a name was bad luck, so I let Sammy name it. After going out fishing one rainy day, it started collecting puddles of water underneath our feet. That's what happens to boats in the rain, but that was enough inspiration for Sammy to figure out what he wanted to name my boat and his new puppy when he got him a few weeks later.

Sammy was wild then and still is, but Puddles' tail looks like it's going to shake off as he's lathering me up both sides of my face with that humongous tongue that he has. Abby reached down to pet him and started playing with him. Puddles was the sweetest dog, but I guess being ever-influenced by three brothers who were always into something wore off on him too. We got him from the local shelter, and, for whatever reason, Sammy picked him out because he peed on him.

I guess that wiz was puppy language for, *take me home, please* and Sammy must have received his signal because that's the one he chose. When we first brought him home, he was just like an infant. We held him like a baby and he'd let you do just about anything you wanted to him as long as he could sleep while you were doing it. Sammy's favorite thing to do with Puddles was wave his little furry legs around like he was a fuzzy beauty queen but, unfortunately, that only lasted a few weeks and then that once sweet little puppy turned into a garbage deposal.

That little thing not only chewed but ate any and everything. I can't count how many times we had to help his backside release a sock or an extension cord. It was nasty. How he lived through his puppyhood is still a wonder to me. Not only because of what he ate, but also because of how many of our father's shoes he devoured. My dad got up really early for work every morning and he always got dressed and tried to leave the house as quietly as he could because the rest of us were still asleep and he didn't want to wake us up. He also always put his shoes by the door.

I can't count the times that we were woken up at 4:00 a.m. by hearing the words, "Damn dog!" Sometimes, Puddles would just hide one or maybe both of my dad's shoes, but other times, he'd fill them up with slobber or chew them to shreds. I don't know why my dad wouldn't stop leaving his shoes by the door but, until that dog got older, I really thought his life was in danger. That dog was a jokester like Sammy too. Our favorite meal, like many younger people's, was pizza. That dog probably took a hundred slices out of our hands. He even once took a slice right out of my mouth before I could get a good bite on it.

Again, like Sammy, he loved water too. We had to take him on every fishing trip we went on, even though he'd never stay in the boat or on the shore. His biggest splash though was the bathtub. If any of us started the water, whether a bath or shower, he'd get in for us and play around, just like he was at the river. This dog was so smart that, after he played in the water as much as he wanted or until we kicked him out, he had his own towel that he'd spread out with his mouth and roll around on until he felt he was dry enough.

I never understood how he could be so dumb to eat things like a TV antenna or a shoe, and then turn around and be smart enough to know how to, not only dry himself off, but lay a towel out to do it. One time he got into some chocolate. I've always heard that chocolate was bad for dogs, but I don't believe it because, after Puddles confiscated quite a bit of it, he was obviously feeling really good—Cheech and Chong kind of good. After calling the vet, the first thing he recommended was to try and make him vomit. How do you make a dog that can eat anything vomit? So, that suggestion was pretty much out of the window.

Then he said try to make him have a bowel movement. All of us shook our head with that proposal too because the dog already crapped all the time, because he ate all the time. I thought chocolate helped with that anyway. The vet then said that chocolate can cause psychedelic reactions in some dogs and, of course, that's the reaction Puddles chose. That poor dog looked like one of those cool hounds on the velvet posters in a pool hall. I was waiting for him to go get some sunglasses and maybe even a cigarette to prop up in his mouth.

It took that little stoner about three days to come down from that high and I think he'd been looking for chocolate ever since. He was a fun dog, but he lived with a fun family, so he didn't have much of an option. As much as we were into, he was always right there by our sides. When Sammy died, Puddles was the first to let us know that something was very wrong. One of the saddest things I've ever seen in my life was how he laid his head on Sammy's chest before the coroner came to our house to get my little brother.

He wouldn't move when they got there either. Puddles never came close to biting anyone, but he almost did when those men came close to someone he loved as much as he loved Sammy. It was so good to see our little buddy. He was definitely as much a part of our family as any of the rest us were, especially after he learned how to leave my father's shoes alone. I heard a whistle and Puddles perked his ears up and ran towards his calling. I didn't know where he was, but I knew it had to be Sammy out there somewhere.

Sammy was the only person that Puddles would leave me for, and that was the way it was supposed to be. I got Puddles for Sammy because I knew he'd miss me when I was away at college. Sammy didn't live too far into my college years and Puddles became everyone's after that. As weird as it sounds, I think I left Puddles for him and he left Puddles for all of us. What a great dog.

My Favorite Angel

If little Miss Abigail wasn't bouncing off the walls before, she definitely was after playing with Puddles. That dog had that effect on everyone, especially children. Being with Abby made me think about Mia, but Abby required so much attention by just being her adventurous little self that it really was pretty hard to do anything else other than just be with her. I didn't mind, though. To be honest, I think that's what people mean when they say to be, "in the moment." Abby made it impossible to do anything other than be in the moment.

This was a pretty long day, and I think she's very glad she stashed that painting somewhere before we went out and about like we did. She really would have crashed after carrying that around all day. Thinking about how funny time is between here and there, I knew when I got a chance to see Mia again, she'd probably be a senior citizen, but something came over me where I felt like I had to look down on her right then. I felt like I did when she hit her eye on the marble table with the babysitter. Abby acted as if she was greatly honored that I asked her to do it with me, so we looked.

As I saw Mia again, this time she wasn't on a front porch getting ready to go to a dance, or even jumping in the house to avoid a St. Bernard. She was driving down the highway. That daggone boy was with her again but, thankfully, he had a hat on, so I didn't have to see that hair stub that looked like Puddles' tail anymore. As they drove, I could tell that things must have gotten a bit more serious with them. It was more of a grown-up conversation about where they'd like to live someday and how many kids they may want. Abby was giggling at me as I shook my head. I think they were even playfully picking out baby names.

I felt this time I was tuning into some sappy soap opera but then it registered to me that this was my own daughter spewing out this hallmark moment stuff. I can't say I didn't want these things for her but, like everything else that has ever happened in life—even in death—I definitely wasn't ready for it. With no exaggeration, I feel like I've been at this place no more than a week or two and now my child is talking about having children and traveling across the world.

I'd ask where the time went, but it seems it went here, and this place is slowly collecting it all. Abby then tugs on my shirt to get my attention on something I didn't see before; it was a silver Honda. I knew I had a feeling that something wasn't quite right with Mia, but she sounded like she was as happy as she's ever been. That silver car was evidentially going to try and change things, though. The car looked as if it had been in three or four wrecks already. It had deep scratches and fresh dents down both of its sides. It also had a spiderwebbed windshield and it was missing one of the side view mirrors.

When it slammed into Mia's car entering the highway, I knew why I had the feeling that I had to see her. My heart sank to a place it had never been. This wasn't just a little fender bender; it was a horrific accident that caused Mia's car to flip over several times and catch on fire with Mia and Wayne inside. I felt I knew what to do in a way, but nothing would work because what overwhelmed me more than anything else was fear for them and rage for the driver of the silver Honda. Abby held my hand as tight as she could and wouldn't let go. No matter how hard I tried to help them, I was helpless.

I was going to have to be forced to see Mia and her friend burn up inside of a car. This would have been the worst thing I would have ever had to see, and I've seen pure evil before. Not once did it register with me where she would most likely go if she didn't survive the accident; I just wanted her to live. All I saw was every vision I had of her life flashing before my eyes. The car seemed like it was rolling in slow motion and I could feel the heat from the flames on every inch of my body. Watching this was like I'd imagine hell to be. Abby didn't leave my side as she closed her eyes with every roll of the car and truck her little chin down at the flames.

She evidentially couldn't help either because she was so scared, even though she was trying every bit as hard as I was. I just knew that my baby girl was dead after the car settled and the flames continued. As breathless as I was by this time, she had to be more so. Other drivers began getting out of their cars and running over to where they had to feel they'd be witnessing a fatality. People tried to get close to the car to see if there was any chance for those inside, but no one could help.

No one except for one man. He was a black man in tattered clothes and an old fatigue military jacket. Somehow, the flames or the carnage of the wrecked car didn't affect him in the least as he dragged my beautiful daughter and her young friend out of the car and laid their motionless bodies on the side of the road. After a few more minutes, the ambulance and police arrived. A few more minutes later, Wayne sat up. He was still in shock of what happened but when he gathered enough of his bearings together, he ran over to Mia and leaned over her lifeless body and prayed. That boy prayed so much.

Not being smart enough to make my own prayers work at first, Abby and I joined in and started praying with him. Then every person or angel, or whatever they were from the reunion on the hill, came almost instantly by our side and started praying with us as well. Then Sammy and my grandparents came too. There was already a mass of people praying for one common goal when my military buddies came to join us. The last to person to get to this glorious congregation was a black man in an old military fatigue jacket. It was Sarge.

What he did for me a hundred times before, he did for my precious daughter as well. We all prayed like we never prayed before. They say where there are two or three gathered in my name, there I am among you. Now, I've heard a lot of things since I got here that wasn't exactly like what I was originally told. I've also seen things here that were completely different than what I ever expected them to be, but, instead of two or three, we had what looked like hundreds praying for Mia and, on that day, everything was just the way it was promised, and our prayers were answered.

No words spoken or ever created could adequately express the gratitude in my heart for everyone who helped pray for Mia. I never felt this full of what I can only describe as pure love and appreciation. This wasn't a numbness at all; this was gratitude in its purest form for an answered prayer. I never thought for one second if the accident would have gone another way that she'd be with me again. I wanted her to live and have a life that, for whatever reason, I wasn't able to finish with her. She had a concussion and minor things that healed in a short amount of time, but she was okay; she was alive.

Sarge didn't stick around after our prayer gathering too long. I guess he had to change clothes again. Even here, he's what he's always been to my life, my favorite angel. That accident solidified Mia and Wayne's fate in a much different way than I saw coming. I guess they had so many things in common, to include both being saved by a man in an old fatigue military jacket, that neither one of them could imagine not spending the rest of their lives together. Wayne had decided to ask Mia to marry him.

After seeing him pray for Mia, and doing something there that I couldn't do here, I knew she'd always be in good hands. Like I've been saying all along, I really like that boy. I laughed to myself as I thought about what started as a very influenced dog attack to where they are now. I don't know why things happen the way they do but, sometimes, they really do end up better than any of us can actually plan for ourselves. I'm humbled by my surroundings like never before. I don't seem to have one foot in the other world and one foot in this one as much as I did before. This place's cleansing methods may not be easy at times, but they sure are working.

In fact, not as much as Miss Grace, but, just maybe, I believe I have a little glow about myself to a greater degree than before. Man, this place is odd but it's a glorious oddity. Abby and I were so happy after the outcome of our assembly that she rarely left my side. We played in the fields and on the path. I told her stories almost like a father does to his beloved daughter. She'd listen as if she was the main character in every tale, especially when I told the story about the great pirate ship, The Armageddon.

We'd even come across some paint and easels in the woods now and then and we'd just let the cerulean blue take us where it would. I knew Mia was more than fine now. I felt like everybody I used to worry about were as well, so I just felt a freedom come over me that I never let myself feel before. Abby drove a lot of those feelings with her curiosity and interest in everything. Mia brought the best out of me there, but Abby's doing that for me here, without question. The best here is different than anywhere else, though.

A person's best here is ridiculously good. The kind of good that creates paintings, waterfalls, angel's wings and even old military fatigue jackets out of nothing except faith and love. There's definitely a learning process, but if I can do it, anyone can. It's amazing. It's a blessed creation in action is what it is.

W-A-Y-N-E

I guess it was bound to happen at some point and, in truth, I'm really happy it's with a young man like Wayne. If it's possible to feel old in a place like this, then that's what I'm feeling. Wayne did everything and even more than anyone would have ever expected of him. He asked for Emily's permission for Mia's hand in marriage. He asked my parents and he even asked my brother, Jacob, as well. That had to be an uncomfortable situation for him. Without me being there, Jacob graciously did many of the fatherly duties throughout the years, and I can't imagine how that conversation went.

Well, yes, I can, because I can see it. Jacob, even being a little older now, is kind of an intimidating-looking fella. He's like our grandfather in the sense that he's more of the gentle type than anything else, but he doesn't look it. He wasn't as chiseled as Sammy's newer appearance is or as big as my grandfather was, but I think if he wanted to be, he could be quite a force to be reckoned with. As Wayne arrived at Jacob's house, the questioning began almost as soon as he came in the door. It was all out of fun, but I don't think Wayne knew that at first.

My brother asked the normal questions that were really none of his business but were asked anyway. He asked where they were going to live, where he was going to work, where they met, etc., etc., etc. He asked all the "where are you" questions until he ran out of them and made it to the question that meant the most. This question stumped Wayne at first; he even had his own eyebrow raised to the sky trying to respond. Jacob asked if he was ever going to give Mia's heart a tummy ache. Wayne was stumped at first thinking about the human anatomy, but once it registered to what Jacob was asking, he smiled with absolute surety in himself and said, "Never."

That young man didn't say no. He didn't hesitate with his answer once he understood the question and he didn't doubt the truth of his words. Jacob didn't just ask that question out of the blue. On the many days after I died, Jacob would pick Mia up and take her to her favorite restaurant, McDonald's, as often as he could, just like me and her did. He was as there for Mia as anyone could be because he knew how she felt.

I saw Jacob break down a hundred times in his car on the way home after dropping Mia off. A lot of this came from another question that he'd often ask my little girl. On many occasions, before he left, he'd ask Mia if she felt better, and nine times out of ten, she'd say, "No, Uncle Jacob. My heart has a tummy ache." Those words would melt anyone's heart as it often did Jacob's. Jacob may have been joking around with the other questions, but that question was no joke to him, or really to any of us. Jacob appreciated and believed the confidence that Wayne had in the young couple's future and, with tears in his own eyes, looked up at me as if I he already knew I was watching.

He shook his head up and down as to show me that he was giving approval for both of us. Mia had no doubt in her future husband's sincerity either and she knew way before this point. I think we all knew some things are just meant to be, even if we don't understand how they became that way. With both of these young people losing their fathers at such a young age, it confusingly helped in a way also.

It helped those two create a bond from a commonality that may never have been able to happen any other way. Another shared lesson they learned together happened after the accident. They both learned, with absolute certainty, that prayer can help them find their way through any challenge that life may present. I even think that Wayne realizes that there is no greater bond than family himself, regardless where some of them may be. I now know we have a new family member coming who will be just as welcomed as the rest. Life has been strange, and this place, my place, has been odd, but right then, both here and there, everything seemed absolutely perfect.

I'm Always with You

Once Abby heard the news about my real daughter getting married, she ran around like she was going to be attending the nuptials live and in-person. She told me that she needed to find an absolutely perfect gift for the occasion. I didn't have the heart to tell her that I think we'd be sitting in the cheap seats, so I let her continue to run around and do what she was doing to find that gift. I don't think anyone ever considered this place to be the cheap seats before, but I really did want us to be there in the way Abby was thinking we would be. If I couldn't be there in-person, I wanted to do something so special for Mia that she'd finally understand that death itself couldn't stop me from being a part of her very special day. That's the connection that kind love can bring.

I wish Miss Grace could be here with me and Abby too. She'd know what to do and probably be just as proud as any grandmotherly-type woman ever was. It didn't take but what felt like a few minutes in their time for it be their wedding day. I still hadn't completely figured out exactly how I was going to do something special for Mia, but I was trying to rack my brain.

This couldn't be anything that was just special though. It had to show Mia, without any doubt, that it's from me, here. I think as it does, fate, something, or someone steps in and always seems to help me out and, once again, it was my brother, Jacob. Now, when I got married, we were kind of broke. We didn't have much of anything but a hope and a prayer, and we didn't seem to do very well with that, but Jacob had his own idea. I've never heard of this before, but he planned a money dance at the reception. Some call it a dollar dance, but I'm glad he didn't use those terms because I didn't want his efforts sounding like a strip club. It was a good idea, though.

It may help them get started a little and I know it would be much appreciated as well. The thing is, Jacob had his own little twist on his version of the money dance; he used two-dollar bills. He set up a hidden table like a horse race bookie and gave everybody who came in two-dollar bills for their singles and loose change. It must have been about five or six thousand dollars' worth of two-dollar bills that were getting ready to be distributed to the unknowing soon-to-be newlyweds.

I don't think I could come up with anything any better, but it wasn't from me. Not to sound petty, but I wanted my gift to Mia to truly be from me. It didn't have to be an expensive gift, it didn't have to be new or blue or any of that other stuff either, it just had to be from me. Abby, from wherever she got it, put on the cutest little dress, as if she was going to be one of the flower girls. Her prior excitement for the day was now replaced with a calm, almost guilty look, as if she was hiding something.

When Mia started walking down the aisle, she had that look on her face that I'd always wished she'd have. She was completely and thoroughly happy. Her mother walked her down by the arm. She had been her father and mother in many ways for so long now, so that definitely made the most sense, and it was a great gift to Emily as well. As she approached Wayne, his knees might have been knocking a little, but Mia's smile eased his nerves as they began exchanging their vows. Mia was so grown and beautiful, but, more importantly, so happy too.

As the final I dos were said and the rice, or whatever is thrown nowadays, there were plans for the reception to be at the military club down the street from the church. With Wayne being somewhat frugal, it was fairly inexpensive, and, in his way, a way to give tribute to his own father. As the couple left the church, Mia jumped in excitement for what she saw that Wayne rented to drive them to the reception and beyond in. It wasn't a limousine, and it wasn't a stretch hummer or anything like that either. It was a little, red convertible Corvette. Wayne knew all her stories, including the one about the Corvette. My heart filled again as I heard my daughter's new husband tell her, "Claim it, girl. Claim it."

As they sped off, I knew this day was great. It was more than great; it was blessed. Mia and Wayne drove that sleek little convertible Corvette around for a while to give everyone time to get to the reception hall before they did. I wasn't watching where they went but, wherever it was, they switched drivers in route because it was Mia who pulled up in the driver's seat at the reception hall, and the tires on that thing looked a little slicker than when they left.

After the first newlywed dance, Mia was noticing that everyone was digging in their pockets for something. That something meant it was time for the money dance. When Mia saw all those two-dollar bills being pinned to her and Wayne, she cried with a humble appreciate and an everlasting remembrance. She knew I couldn't help when I had to leave, but she also knew that I was never very far away either. Jacob and the rest of their guests outdid themselves and the happy little bride became even happier. I could have sworn that she was so happy, she was even glowing.

Most new couples need money—that's a given—but Mia didn't care about how much the many two-dollar bills they received added up to. She cared what they stood for. She cared that her daddy said with that many two-dollar bills, her wishes in life would be limitless. They'd be limitless for her, but also for her own new family too.

My Simple Gift

As the couple moved to the gift table, there was a big rectangular box leaning across the back of the table with a tablecloth laid across it instead of it being wrapped with wrapping paper like all the other presents. I'd been a little nosy before, so I knew what most of the presents were, but even I didn't know what was inside this big box. Mia went over and tugged on the corner until the tablecloth covering it slid to the floor. As she did, she put both of her hands up to her mouth in astonishment at what I'm guessing is the same reaction I had to the first time I saw cerulean blue.

It was the painting. I knew it, and my little partner in crime, Abby, knew it too because she was the one who made sure it was there on Mia's special day. That guilty look that Abby was trying to hide before turned to one of extreme satisfaction with herself now. It was a deserving look too because I was just as grateful for her thinking so much about Mia, but also about me.

What I couldn't do myself, my new little buddy did without me having a clue. I was so grateful for this little girl who seemed to be with me all the time now too. I may have not found the perfect present for Mia's wedding, but she did. The new painting that Abby hid somewhere in the woods came out at the perfect time. It was more or less an exact copy of the original that I painted, but no one would ever know. Mia never knew the story of that painting, but my parents and Jacob did. When they saw the tablecloth drop and my painting underneath, they all looked at each other as to say, "Did you do that?"

After confirmation, they realized that it didn't come from any of them, and they too received a confirmation, even if it was from Abby, that I'd be with them, and I always will. I think my parents and Jacob should save that story for Mia. Life is full of ups and downs, and maybe the best time to tell it to her is when she needs it the most. She's okay. She's more than fine now. She's very, very happy.

I have no right feeling any other way than grateful, not a bit, but I do. I want something from just me to her. I know it sounds selfish, but I feel I need to do it for both of us. The reception hall had two sides, one, of course, is where Mia and Wayne's wedding reception was being held. It was also where it was just about to end, allowing the couple to race off in that beautiful Corvette once more. On the other side was another large room that was already being set up for a birthday party, a little girls seventh birthday party, to be specific. The birthday event crew started bringing in the games and cake and all kinds of things that a seven-year-old would like.

As the next party delivery truck pulled up, the driver got out and asked the man who was obviously in charge where he wanted that load dropped off. I could tell that the boss man was stressed and evidentially working on a deadline that they might not meet, so he yelled out, "Door two! Take the stuff to door two, and hurry up!" Now, one side of this reception hall was Mia's party and the other was door two where the birthday party was going to be.

Once the man backed to the door and opened the back of his truck, I knew what I wanted my special wedding gift to my precious daughter to be, even if I had to borrow it from a seven-year-old. I didn't know if I could do it myself, and I knew it would be such a little thing compared to the many wonderful things they received that day, to include my painting from Abby, but this idea was special to me because It was going to be directly from me. The delivery driver didn't take kindly to being yelled at or told to hurry up, so when he made his delivery, he just opened the door and started flinging what he brought in the first door he came to.

He threw one after the other until they were all inside and then drove off in disgust at how he'd been treated. Now, this part I didn't do; that was the something or someone looking out for me again, but the next move was all mine. The reception hall had big fans in each corner because, although there was air conditioning, it could still get quite hot with so many people inside dancing, and, in some cases, jumping all around, but they were so loud that someone went around and turned them all off.

After the frustrated delivery man left his load in the entry way to Mia's reception instead of inside of door two, I decided to have a come to Jesus meeting with the fans to cut them back on. It finally worked! It seems that little girl who was getting ready to have a birthday party loved balloons, I mean really loved them, because there must have been a thousand of those things already blown up and ready to go. Where I was helped once more was that her favorite color was evidentially green as well, just like me, and just like those balloons that Mia released for me so many years ago.

When those fans kicked on, they pushed all those green balloons to where everyone was at the wedding reception, to include Mia. There were hundreds and hundreds of floating green acknowledgments of our eternal connection floating around the room everywhere. There were so many balloons that they seemed to be coming up through the floor and pleasantly invading almost every inch of that joyous gathering. To me and Mia, it was a definite present that told her that her daddy was still with her, and always will be too.

Mia looked in amazement because she remembered what she had done for me so long ago in a very similar fashion. Now she knows with certainty that her prayers were answered. It may have only been balloons, but I don't think I could have given her a more fitting or conformational present. As the couple finally got to the door to leave, Mia at first acted as if she never wanted that particular time of that magical day to end. Then she remembered, as she gathered all the green balloons that would fit inside that little red car, that her daddy would always be with her.

Mia tweaked the tires of that jet car one more time while both husband and wife were waiving out the window. Mia waived from the driver's side and Wayne was proud that she was. Have you ever had those days where you're almost too happy to move? This was similar to when I got to this place because I was definitely in some sort of self-imposed trance, but instead of having any feelings of doubt or confusion, all I felt was overwhelming joy.

There was no question about where I was anymore because there couldn't be any other place that could provide such a blessed day as this place just did. This time, instead of doing all I knew how to do, we all thanked God so much from both here and there and everywhere. There was so much thanks.

True Grace

Abby was so proud of herself and I was proud of her too. She gave Mia and I the perfect gift. I miss Miss Grace and often wonder where she is, but if I had to have another heavenly companion, I couldn't think of any better company than this little girl. *This place is odd, oddly perfect*, I thought. This time, instead of us rambling around the path in the woods and through the flowers as we've been doing, Abby said she had to take me somewhere again. The last time we had to go to a specific place at a specific time, we ended up in a family reunion with eons of different generations in attendance, so there was no telling where this new destination would be.

As we went to get back on the path, I noticed there wasn't a path to get on, it had finished. I was so used to the ever-growing brightness and the music that I didn't realize that this part of my journey was going to end. I understood enough to know that the journey was the real destination, but what could be next? Miss Grace told me God was everything because in everything was his love, so, was I going to meet everything?

I too, along with everyone around me, had been glowing a little more for a while now but when we arrived at the next destination, almost everything, to include us, was pure light. Instead of being a resting place, Abby called it a thanking place. I asked if she meant thinking and just country twanged her 'i,' but she giggled and said, "No, Grampy, a thanking place. She didn't tell me what I was supposed to do. I think she wanted me to figure out for myself as she left me alone to do so. I guess she figured by the name she gave me that I could at least do that. This place was so radiant and bustling with brilliance. It was so peaceful too with this particular hymn permeating everything.

I felt that I had already thanked God, thanked him so much, and I meant it too. I was given much, and I even learned how to help a little, even if it was just with a few fans. I didn't have a problem dropping to my knees to give thanks again, so I did. I gave thanks for my brothers and Jacob's family. I gave thanks for my grandparents and parents. I also gave thanks for Sarge and my buddies, my many family members from the reunion over the hill, and Nasim and the men from the old concrete building too.

Of course, I gave thanks for my Mia and her new husband. I thanked God so much for any and everything that ever happened to me and for me. I could have gone on all day because, for one, time here is funny, but also because I had so much to be thankful for. I was finally completely lost in that place, but the good kind of lost where you know the outcome is going to be so much better than anybody or even yourself could have planned. When I opened my eyes, almost everyone that I was with on this journey was surrounding me. Sarge and his tattered wings was there, Sammy with what looked like a sublease contract in his hands, my reunion family, my grandparents, and Nasim and his men were all there too.

It looked like when everyone came to help pray for Mia but, this time, it was for me. In the back of all those gathered people in that holiest of holy lights were a few people who I hadn't seen before, but I could tell we were related as well. Maybe not by a bloodline but by something much greater, and they were the ones who evidentially called this meeting. The one who was a bit brighter than the others—if that was possible—called me over to him.

I had to look like a little star going over to meet the brightest planet. When I got to him, everything shook as he placed his hands on my shoulders like Sarge used to do. At first, I thought he was going to call me Rain in the Sky, but that's not what happened, thankfully. When he gently placed his hands on my shoulders, everything single thing that ever happened in my life and afterlife, both good and bad, flashed through my mind all at once. All the memories that I ever had were gone after that for a brief time. They didn't leave my mind forever, but they had no place around such greatness.

I was in total peace, surrounded by total love. As my memories slowly returned, they didn't have the same control over me. They were there, but like the tattoos I used to have on my arm, they were diminished when they came in contact with the extra amazing light. This was to be my final welcoming party of sorts. The actual acceptance and approval for being able to be where I am. Strangely, I was in the full acknowledgment that it wasn't me who had to do anything at all. If I thought green balloons were the ultimate gift for Mia, it was absolutely nothing compared to knowing what was given to me and to everyone, everywhere through true grace.

Grampy

As we concluded, the man who grabbed my shoulders earlier went out of sight. I knew he left because I saw him leave but I still felt him right there with me. I learned that day that he always would be with me too. Even though I felt different and even realized that I was looking at things a little differently, I still knew that Miss Grace, and now Abby, were missing in action. I don't know what else these people could be doing that could be any more important than what just happened, but, with my new way of looking at things, I know whatever they are doing is going to be wonderful.

The others didn't seem to leave, they just stayed gathered together like you would at any reunion. *Even with this additional glow, this place is so odd*, I thought. Everyone talked and I had to make sure that Sammy didn't think we'd actually be moving in together for sure. As Sammy and I were standing together, my grandparents came over too. As my family surrounded me, there was another light that came from where the supremely majestic man was standing earlier. This light was a bit different. It almost looked like the brightest sparkler that floated and spiraled around, eventually landing in my hands.

I looked at my family as to say I didn't know they had fireworks here. They just smiled and said it was time to see Mia again. This time, I led us to see her and instead of having any fear or feelings that anything was wrong. I knew that there were plans for her and I knew they were much greater than even I, her father, this father, could ever give her. As I looked down, with my family and friends all tightened around me, what I saw put me on my knees. Time here is still funny, but it seems that funny time almost made me miss that sparking light leave my hands and circle all around this place, soaking up so much of its glory and that pure love that was all around, and I myself truly just felt.

The sparkle didn't stay around here long, though, because it was being called somewhere else. It was being called to Mia. Once that sparkle lovingly blended into its future, Mia went into labor for about two hours. Wayne was right there by her side being exactly who I knew he would be. Neither one of us smoked, but I think we both could have used a cigarette at that point. As this precious sparkly gift breathed its first breath, both looked up and smiled. Their thanks weren't directed at me or even to Wayne's father who was also in our blessed crowd of onlookers now.

It was lovingly given to whom gave that little truly perfect package to them. They already had the baby's name picked out. I'm sure they probably came up with it on that original ride that I eavesdropped on. As the nurse was cleaning up that precious little girl, she swaddled the baby snuggly in a blanket that, without a doubt, was made in a very familiar color. She then gently handed the baby wrapped so lovingly in that regal amber blanket to her new parents. For some reason, nurses always seem to feel they need to introduce the new little babies to their parents. This wonderful nurse was no different as she said, "Mommy and daddy, meet your new little girl, little Miss Grace Abigail."

All the light, love and music exploded at once. It was like the fourth of July had a fourth of July, and I thanked God so much once again; we all did, and if possible, greater than ever before. I may have been slow at times, but I knew this little girl was my granddaughter and I knew Abigail and Miss Grace would always know it too. As I saw the new addition to my family in the arms of my greatest blessing, I knew more than ever I was with them and I always will be too!

May God Bless You

www.ingramcontent.com/pod-product-compliance
Lightning Source LLC
Chambersburg PA
CBHW061205170626
46809CB00003B/1248